I0738594

GRANDMOTHER'S DEVIL

&

OTHER TEMPTING TALES

GRANDMOTHER'S DEVIL

&

OTHER TEMPTING TALES

MARTY MALIN

ILLUSTRATED BY DIANE SLADE

Copyright © 2020 Harold Martin Malin Jr.

All rights reserved
Printed in the United States of America
First Edition, 2020

No part of this book may be reproduced or transmitted in any form or by any means, electronic or mechanical, including photocopying, recording, or by any information storage or retrieval system, without the written permission of the author, except for reviewers who may quote brief passages.

Published by Canyon Rose Press
Benicia, California

email: info@canyonrosepress.com
www.canyonrosepress.com

Any resemblances to actual persons, living or dead, and enterprises, settings or locales, historical or contemporary, are entirely coincidental and are either the product of the author's imagination or are used fictitiously.

Publisher's Cataloging-in-Publication Data

Names: Malin, Marty, author. | Slade, Diane, illustrator.
Title: Grandmother's devil & other tempting tales / Marty Malin; illustrated by Diane Slade.
Description: Benicia, CA: Canyon Rose Press, 2020.
Identifiers: ISBN 978-1-7343827-1-6 (pbk.) | 978-1-7343827-2-3 (epub) | 978-1-7343827-0-9 (audio)
Subjects: LCSH Grandmothers--Fiction. | Older women--Fiction. | Short stories, American. | BISAC FICTION / Short Stories (single author) | FICTION / Women
Classification: LCC PS3613 .A38 G73 2020 | DDC 813.6--dc23

Ideas come and go, stories stay.

NASSIM NICHOLAS TALEB

For my grandmothers

Sophia Alice Malin (1892-1973)

Lydia Ann Haines (1904-1997)

CONTENTS

An old woman floats easily between worlds, none of them in as sharp relief as they once were. She spends her last hours on her front porch, resting in her white wicker rocker, sipping lemonade from her favorite glass, the one with the stenciled lemon slices.

A dissolute young man is brought up short by a vintage automaton he has painstakingly restored. An eerie fortune-telling session drives him into the street naked and stark-raving mad. Who, indeed, is that nurse in the mental hospital?

Hannah writes the story of her grandson's life and excruciating death at the hands of occupying Romans, a testament against the lies of foolhardy rebels and zealots that grow ever more fantastic in the retelling.

49   GRANDMOTHER, NAKED

A widow finds new meaning to her life as a model for a college life drawing class, only to find illicit nude photos and degrading tweets have been posted online. She takes her revenge.

71   GRANDMOTHER'S DEVIL

An otherworldly being watches over a comatose grandmother molested by an unscrupulous nurse. Grandmother's Devil intends to drag the nurse's soul screaming into hell, but Grandmother has other plans.

89   GRAND-MÈRE LE CIGARE

A cigar-rolling Cuban virgin becomes the matriarch of a Napa Valley dynasty, having seduced a French brandy maker seeking his fortune in America. She shepherds her grandson from humiliating failure to a fairy-tale marriage to his childhood sweetheart.

GRANDMOTHER SITS

Grandmother sits in the fraying white wicker chair on a warm September late afternoon, on the wraparound porch, a few feet from her open screened front door.

She sits on the comfortable cushion she covered with material from a pair of faded curtains printed with bluebells that used to hang in the spare bedroom. Now the bedroom has lace curtains. The lace is yellowing, but it lets in more light, so the room is more cheerful and inviting, Grandmother thinks.

Grandmother's sugared iced tea, in her favorite glass with the stenciled lemon slices, rests on the painted wrought iron table beside her, next to the Mason jar filled with fragrant lilacs she picked this morning. The ice in her tea has almost melted.

She sits with eyes lightly closed, slumped against the curving wicker backrest, her head with its swept-back silver-white hair tilting downward, chin resting between the top button of her dress and the yoke of her home made green gingham apron, her ample breasts sloping toward her soft belly.

Her veiny hands, the skin soft and translucent from a nightly slathering of Porcelana, are nested in her lap where her embroidered handkerchief has come to rest, slipping from her gnarled fingers.

Grandmother floats easily between worlds, most of them pleasant, none of them in as sharp relief as they used to be. When she was a young girl, born in this very house, Luther Goodman's family lived in a fine Georgian-style home up the road. There were only five houses along the entire road then, just a gravel road into town interrupting the limitless prairie, with the houses set back a piece. Luther's home looked out of place, despite the stately old sycamores in the front yard.

"Not a decent prairie home at all," her Ma would grouse from time to time. "I guess some folks just have to put on airs."

All the other houses except Grandmother's are gone now, replaced by modest ranch-style homes along streets and cul-de-sacs branching off a broad paved boulevard that replaced the old gravel road.

Most everything changed after the War. The missile defense base a few miles away, with its underground silos, brought new schools and a large shopping mall west of the old downtown. It is Grandmother's house that now looks out of place.

There's not much left of the old town anymore. The dull brick City Hall and the marble-faced Midland Bank Building, now home to a law firm and a title company, still stand facing each other on the north and south sides of Pioneer Square with its four WWI canons pointing outward from a central bronze statue of "The Frontier Woman," babe in arms and two children in tow, striding resolutely westward.

From the east side of the square, the fine neo-gothic Methodist church and campanile, built of limestone quarried in neighboring Kendall County, keep watch over "The Frontier Woman" and her brood on their sojourn. But most of the businesses that thrived around Pioneer Square during Grandmother's youth have long-since closed.

Luther's family had one of the first Plymouths ever made. His father would sometimes pass Grandmother and her family walking along the road and offer them a ride, but Ma and Grandma always politely declined. "No, thank you kindly," they would say. And later, as they walked, they would repeat a familiar litany among themselves. "Too fine a day to be cooped up in a car," they would say, even if the weather was a bit unsettled. "A little rain (or snow, or wind) never hurt nobody. Prairie folks got no need for fancy automobiles," they would say. "Nothing wrong with riding on shanks' mare."

Sometimes, when Luther got older, his father let him drive the Plymouth on a weekend as he coached from the back seat. Luther would toot the horn and give a cheery wave. Grandmother would pretend not to notice.

But one warm autumn day like today, as Luther was driving the Plymouth, this time without his father, he passed Grandmother walking by herself along the gravel road. He stopped the car and waited for her to catch up.

"Rose Marie," he said, wearing a goofy grin, "I declare I have asked you time and again to take a ride with me. You gonna break my heart again today? You gonna keep on turning me down?"

"Luther Goodson," Grandmother said not unkindly. "I reckon I'll take a ride into town with you today if that will stop you from pestering me." Luther's soft brown eyes twinkled as he smiled and held the passenger door open for her.

"I ain't makin' no promises," he chuckled.

Grandmother settled herself into the supple leather seat. Luther got in behind the steering wheel and started the engine. "Not too fast now," she said. "I wouldn't like it if you went too fast." Luther motored gently along the road.

"Where you off to today, Rose Marie?" Luther asked.

"I'm just going to the Five and Dime for some more crochet thread. I'm almost finished with the pillow slips I'm making for Ma's birthday next week and I've run out of her favorite blue."

"I've got to pick Dad up at the bank," Luther said. "We could give you a ride home when you've finished your shopping if you want."

"Now wouldn't that be something," Rose Marie said, "you driving me up to the house, my Ma looking out the front window. I don't suppose I'd ever hear the end of it once she finished sputtering about what came over me. Thank you kindly, Luther. I'll just walk back home same as I always do."

Luther grinned, pushing a stray lock of hair off his forehead.

Grandmother remembered looking at him closely once or twice as he drove. The fact that it was her first automobile ride hadn't stopped her from noticing that Luther had missed a couple of spots shaving. And there was no mistaking the scent of his father's Bay Rum. A little too much, Grandmother thought, but not altogether unpleasant.

He was handsome, she thought. She remembered it all to

this day: the intoxicating scent of the aftershave mixed with the smell of the Plymouth's elegant leather upholstery, the steady hum of the engine, and the crunch of the gravel beneath the tires.

Luther managed to find other opportunities for Grandmother to ride with him. One evening she was sure she saw her Ma staring at them disapprovingly from behind the curtains. Her Ma never said anything about it though, nor did she forbid Grandmother from riding in the Plymouth. But she thought it her obligation as a parent to pass along a little wisdom about life's pitfalls just in case.

"Remember, child," these admonitions would often begin, "we're not their kind. They're rich folks."

Warming to her task she would say, "They seem nice enough but they're not workin' people like us. His daddy's bank's got the mortgage to our house. And you know that Scripture says it's harder for rich folks to get into heaven than for a camel to go through the eye of a needle.

"Of course, the Psalmist sings to 'Both low and high, rich and poor together,' so I'm sure Heavenly Father has a plan for us all that we won't fully comprehend until we meet Him in Glory!

"Not that we're poor. Not by any means! The Good Lord always provides but sometimes I wonder why He has to cut it so close."

Then came the Senior Prom at the District 11 High School gymnasium and a magnificent corsage, a tentative first kiss followed by Grandmother's smile of encouragement.

The kissing became more frequent and more purposeful in the weeks that followed. Several clumsy attempts at going further were rebuffed, politely but firmly, as was expected of a young woman of Grandmother's upbringing, though her heart was not in it. The summer after graduation, Grandmother accepted Luther's proposal of marriage without the slightest hesitation.

They lived with Grandmother's parents after they were married. In those days, the house sat on much more land with well-tended walnut and fruit trees in abundance. Luther surprised everyone by becoming an eager and accomplished orchardist.

Grandmother's father died unexpectedly the following winter. Her mother, unable to bear living on the orchard without him, moved across town to live with her sister. Grandmother and Luther became the new owners of the property.

The arrival of Luther, Jr., and two years later the twins, Emma and Laura, all born at home, multiplied their happiness. Then Luther went off to war and a hired man helped Grandmother look after the orchard.

On a snowy Saturday afternoon, the following February, two men from the War Office delivered the sad news of Luther's death in combat.

Time passed. The kids went off to college and settled in big cities across the country. Grandchildren followed, visiting during the holidays and school vacations. And now, the grandchildren had children.

* * *

"Ah," Grandmother smiles, without looking up from her reverie. "Here comes Cletus with the mail."

The almost silent electric delivery truck pauses up the street, three houses away at the Yoshimotos, then two doors up at the Hollisters, then finally in front of Grandmother's house.

"Sounds like Cletus has forgotten his push-cart again,"

Grandmother thinks. "That man's going to ruin his back with that heavy bag."

Ruby Mae opens the gate in the low wrought iron fence. "Afternoon, Grandmother," she says, climbing the painted concrete steps to the wraparound porch.

"Oh, Luther, is that you?" Grandmother asks softly, not opening her eyes. "I thought I had lost you. Have you seen the Jewel Tea man? He's usually here by this time with our groceries."

"It's Ruby Mae, Grandmother, with the mail. Not much to deliver today. Here's your Capper's Weekly and the advertising flyer from Rexall. I'll just put them here on the table."

"The table's just fine, thank you" she says, slowly opening her eyes. "Luther will mix it all up if you take it inside. Is Cletus sick today?"

"Cletus retired over a year ago, Grandmother. He's doing fine. Moved away with his wife to Arizona and left me to carry his route. He sent me a Christmas card last year with a Kodak of the mobile home park where he lives. Has a nice, nearly new trailer out there. He reminded me to take extra special good care of you."

"Cletus is a nice man. Tell him I hope he feels better soon and can get back to work. A man has to feed his family. It's so nice of you to help him out until he's better."

"You take care now, Grandmother," Ruby Mae said. "Is there anything you need?"

"No, I'm just fine. Got everything I need right here. Just waitin' for the Jewel Tea. He's such a nice man. Reminds me of my Luther. So handsome!"

"OK, then, Grandmother. Tomorrow's Sunday so I'll see you again Monday afternoon."

Grandmother closes her eyes as Ruby May latches the wrought iron gate. The mail truck glides down the road and stops in front of the Singhs.

"Luther," Grandmother says quietly, "you should come out here and sit on the porch with me. It's such a beautiful time of the day. We can just visit for a minute and then I'll go inside and fix your supper.

"I picked the last of the tomatoes today and there's some of my special cornbread in the skillet. There's leftover ham hocks and navy beans too. We can come back out here later in the cool and have our peach cobbler with cream before bedtime. I got a good scald on that last batch of peaches I put up."

Grandmother sits in the lengthening evening. The setting sun gives way to flashing fireflies and the songs of crickets and cicadas, then to the midnight moon and stars. Grandmother takes no notice.

"It's good to have you back, Luther. I've missed you so! How nice that you brought me my sweet tea in my favorite glass. You always did know just what I liked. But, you know, I think I'd better go up now and rest in bed. Lots doin' tomorrow, what with Church and all."

Grandmother sits with her eyes closed on a bright Sunday morning, slumped in the fraying white wicker chair with the bluebell cushion on her wraparound porch. The screened front door is still open. Her undrunk tea, in the glass with the stenciled lemon slices, still rests on the painted wrought iron table, next to the Mason jar filled with the fading lilacs she picked yesterday morning. She does not see the hummingbird hovering around her petunias, sipping nectar from the velvety red blossoms. Nor does she hear the distant bell in the campanile overlooking Pioneer Square summoning the faithful to worship.

GRANDMOTHER'S PREDICTIONS

Noise from a delivery truck dieseling in front of his house dragged Earle out of a recurring erotic dream involving a much older woman with fire-flecked opalescent eyes. He could never remember the details once he reluctantly gave in to wakefulness. The steamy imagery would evaporate, leaving only his rapidly faltering arousal to validate that he had been engaged in something transcendent and possibly illicit.

The noise from the truck was insistent. Earle untangled himself from Brandy and scrambled out of bed. He made his way over to the bedroom window, pulled apart the narrow slats of his blinds, and squinted into the daylight. No mistake. The driver had turned off the engine and was climbing down from the cab.

Earle scrambled to pull on his underpants and drag yesterday's too-small yellow "Robots Rule, Humans Drool!" tee shirt over his head just seconds before the doorbell rang.

"Back in a jif, Brandykins," he said, heading downstairs toward his front door. "Don't go 'way."

He answered the bell as if it were completely unremarkable that he was only half dressed. The driver pretended not to notice.

"I got a 300-pound crate on the truck for an Earle Winston Bradlee the Third. That you?"

"Yep," Earle replied. "That's me."

"Where you want me to put it, buddy?"

"The driveway's fine," Earle said.

"By rights we're not supposed to take it past the curb, but I don't suppose there's any harm dropping it in the driveway, just so long as we don't have to bring it into the house or nothing," the driver said, trying to keep his eyes on Earle's face and off his pale, scrawny legs. The tee shirt stopped short of covering his underpants completely. Earle stood in his bare feet, scratching his backside absentmindedly.

"Thanks," Earle said.

"Right," the driver said, holding out a beat-up aluminum clipboard. "You'll have to sign for it."

"You guys should get tablets," Earle said, as he reached for the clipboard.

"I guess it's coming to that," the driver grunted. *And maybe you should get some pants.*

"How's about I give you fifty bucks to roll it into the garage as long as you got it on the dolly?" said Earle.

"White Glove Service is an extra hundred bucks," the driver said.

"Well, I'm not exactly asking for White Glove Service. Fifty bucks to just drop it inside the garage instead of the driveway. I'll unpack it myself."

"Sure. Fifty bucks. Why not?"

"Okay. I'll open up. Meet you in the garage."

Earle closed the front door, took the stairs to the bedroom two at a time and quickly pulled on his jeans and sandals. He hustled back downstairs, out the kitchen door leading to the garage and raised the overhead door.

The driver was lowering the lift gate, standing beside the crate already loaded on the hand truck. "Thanks," said Earle, handing the driver the cash once the crate was inside the garage.

"No problem. Have a good one," the driver said, heading towards his truck as Earle lowered the garage door.

Earle went up to the bedroom, ripped off his clothes and crawled back into bed with Brandy.

"The Old Woman has arrived!" he said. He hadn't been this excited since Brandy was wheeled into his garage three months ago.

"Now don't be jealous, Brandykins," he said. "She's nothing like you. You know you're my special girl."

Brandy was indeed special. Earle had specified every detail of her 5'1", 34-24-35 silicone body. She had fair skin dusted with a smattering of freckles and cranberry-to-tangerine ombré hair. Earle had sprung for prosthetic-grade green eyes.

He had ordered a custom wheeled tripod for storage. Leaving her lying down too long would distort her beautiful curves.

"Well," he said to Brandy, getting out of bed for the second time this morning, "I can't just leave the old gal in the garage. Sorry, foxy lady, but you'll have to excuse me." He picked Brandy up, his hands interlocked under her breasts, and positioned her on the tripod next to the bed. Still naked, he padded downstairs through the kitchen into the garage.

A crowbar and mallet made short work of uncrating his new treasure: a life-sized torso in a refrigerator-sized dark oak and glass cabinet trimmed with antique brass.

She was exquisite, despite the fact that her clothes were moth-eaten and her nearly bald head was badly cracked, with a sizeable chunk missing. Still, her elegant Romani face was captivating. Earle was smitten.

When he first spotted her in an on-line auction, he knew he had to have her: a genuine 1929 "Grandmother's Predictions" fortune-teller with the original #29 wax head, hand crafted in Dresden, Germany. She was the automaton of his dreams, the original "Cleveland Grandma," as the cognoscenti called her, built by the now defunct William Gent Vending Company in Cleveland, Ohio.

Over the next few weeks, he restored "Grandmother's Predictions" to her original splendor in his garage workshop. It had been straightforward enough to repair her mechanical action, turning the odd metal part on his lathe, truing up the supporting rod and escapement, rebuilding the motor and refinishing the cabinetry and fittings.

He had done much more complex restorations at the *Musée Mécanique.* He had loved working at the museum, near the old Sutro Baths and the Cliff House, with its lovely old San Francisco feel. Yes, it was out of the way and slightly seedy, but the museum's collections were part of a rundown, slightly seedy past.

Aside from the *Musée Mécanique*, working for a living had never been one of Earle's strengths. He had just managed to graduate from high school. College was out of the question.

His father tried his best, using his business connections, to help Earle "make something of himself." Most of his attempts had failed.

Once he had helped Earle land a job at a bicycle repair shop in the Mission. That lasted for almost three months before Earle decided he'd had enough of sprockets and derailleurs.

A job at an automotive dealership seemed promising, once Earle moved from the sales floor to the grease racks, but Earle found changing oil filters and rotating tires boring. He soon chucked that job as well.

Earle stumbled into the job at the *Musée Mécanique* by accident. As a visitor, he had found the automatons fascinating and he had a talent for spotting small mechanical problems with the machines.

This one had a sudden judder that occurred in a predictable pattern. That one squeaked annoyingly or swallowed his token without delivering the promised performance. Such malfunctions annoyed Earle greatly.

Earle would flag down some hapless employee and direct his attention to the offending machine. He also typically offered his diagnosis and prescribed steps that might be taken to remedy the problem.

Often as not, the response to Earle's careful analysis was to pull the plug and hang an "Out of Order" sign on the machine. When that happened, Earle would demand to speak with the manager. After a few such encounters, the manager decided the best way to get Earle out of his hair would be to hire him. It was the first job Earle had gotten without his father's intervention.

Before long, he was helping with minor repairs and one or two of the craftsmen began to share the secrets of their trade with him. Earle soaked it all up.

He was a natural. Soon, he was able to figure out what was ailing the machines and how to fix even the most complex malfunctions. The *Musée Mécanique* paid Earle only a meager salary but, with a generous subsidy from his father, he moved out of his parents' house into an apartment in North Beach.

Earle's star was on the ascendant. Even better news came on his 25th birthday. On that auspicious day, Earl learned from his grandfather's attorneys that he was a trust fund baby. Earle's grandfather had made a lot of money in the old San Francisco both he and Earle idolized, and Earle had inherited it all. The money would never run out. The first thing he did was to buy a house closer to the *Musée Mécanique* in nearby Sea Cliff.

When the *Musée Mécanique* moved to Fisherman's Wharf, with its slick facades and hordes of gawking tourists, Earle wanted no part of it. He declared himself to be retired at the age of twenty-six.

Earle began to work full-time acquiring and restoring arcade machines for his own collection, which was rapidly taking over his rec room. "Grandmother's Predictions" would be the crown jewel of his personal arcade.

Grandmother's wax head had been the most challenging part to restore. He repaired the crack and replaced the missing piece, building up the wax layers meticulously. He had anchored silvery human hair strand by strand in the wax scalp and swept it back into a bun.

He wanted her clothing to be authentic; it had taken a

bit of time to find suitable fabrics from her era. He had hand stitched a pleated, cream silk blouse and trimmed it with fabric-covered buttons. He had appliqued handmade lace at the throat and the sleeves and draped her shoulders with an antique Belgian lace shawl. A marquise-cut amethyst pendant, teardrop pearl earrings and a gold wedding ring set with a circle of diamonds completed her jewelry. Delicate gold wire-rim spectacles accented her fire-flecked opalescent eyes.

When he was finished, he carefully moved her from the garage to a place of honor in his rec room arcade. When he plugged her in, the motor whirred, and the lights came on. She looked splendid. Until now, his most prized possession had been a triple-monkey barrel organ automaton, featuring a monkey magician and a pair of monkeys playing stringed instruments.

He also had a vintage ESCO "Sex Appeal Meter," a "Popeye Arm Wrestler," and a "Zoltan" fortune-teller. Next to Popeye in the arcade was a 1947 D. Gottlieb & Co. "Humpty Dumpty" pinball machine, the first ever to incorporate flippers.

In a nod to modernity, he had acquired an arcade model "Space Harrier" console. It was flanked by some of his oldest and most beautiful machines, hand-cranked clamshell Mutoscopes from the early 1900s with interchangeable peep show reels.

The Mutoscopes featured such titles as "What the Butler Saw," "After the Bath," and "Late at Night in the Bedroom," all with their original faded advertising cards. He had learned how to make far more explicit reels for these old Mutoscopes with the assistance of Photoshop and YouTube instructional videos. He had even cobbled together a passable Philadelphia Toboggan Company "Laffing Sal" from painted, horsehair strengthened papier-mâché and mechanical parts salvaged from non-functioning units.

Earle's tenure at the *Musée Mécanique* had served him well.

"Grandmother's Predictions" had shipped with a deck of 30 original fortune cards. More were available on eBay, but for now these would do nicely. He unlocked the cabinet concealing Grandmother's mechanical innards and stacked the fortune cards neatly in the dispensing mechanism.

He put a nickel in the brass coin slot near the top of the cabinet and Grandmother came to life. Her hand moved left, then right, then left again, back and forth, hovering above a fan of tarot cards on the baize-covered table in front of her. Her head moved up and down, to one side then the other, fixing Earle with her gaze. Her chest breathed in and out under her silk blouse. And then her hand stopped, hovering above the Queen of Cups. He heard his fortune drop into the brass receptacle with gilt lettering above it announcing "Your Answer Is Here."

Grandmother's Predictions

Worry turns the hair gray and breaks down the health and never yet has done a person any good.

Don't worry over your money matters, just work, work, work. Work will keep your mind off your troubles, make you more cheerful; cheerfulness brings sunshine; sunshine brings happiness; happiness brings a clear mind, and a clear mind brings good work; good work brings good money, and money makes more money.

A bright life is in store for you if you will just work
and work and stop worrying.

Drop Another Nickel in the Slot
and I Will Tell You More

Why not? Earle smiled to himself. He deposited another nickel in the slot and Grandmother began to move again. His fortune was delivered below.

Grandmother's Predictions

Slow methods and hesitant excution of
business affairs will plunge you into deeper
misery if you do not wake up and learn to act
quick. You possess good instinct and fine
business abilities. Beware of people who
approach you with schemes whereby you will
get rich quick.

You are on the road to fame and fortune.
Do not let your opportunity pass you by.

Drop Another Nickel in the Slot
and I Will Tell You More

Earle was beyond happy with his restored automaton. Unlocking the cabinet, he replaced the fortune cards in the dispenser and went up to his bedroom. He peeled off his clothes and dropped them on the floor, lifted Brandy from her tripod and trundled her into his unmade bed.

Unable to sleep, he headed back down the stairs toward the kitchen for a bedtime snack. He polished off a couple of chocolate donuts, grabbed an open carton of milk from the refrigerator and sniffed it. Convinced it had not gone sour, he chugged the dregs straight from the carton, belched, wiped his mouth on the dish towel and went into the arcade.

He cranked one of the Mutoscopes through a homemade porno reel, fondling himself half-heartedly, then giggled good night to "Grandmother's Predictions."

Back in the bedroom, he crawled in beside Brandy.

"Isn't she a marvel, Brandykins? Oh, right! You two haven't met yet. Probably better to keep it that way. But don't ever forget that you are my special girl." He gave one breast a desultory squeeze, rolled over and fell asleep.

Earle rarely bothered to get dressed when he got up and the next morning was no exception. He made himself a mug of coffee, which he gulped standing up, playing a round of Humpty Dumpty Pinball.

He went to the kitchen for a second mug and a chocolate donut and then went back into the arcade for a serious encounter with "Space Harrier."

He rarely got past Level 16. But this time he made it all the way through Level 18. "Yes!" he whooped, pumping the air with his fist. "That's how the game is played, right Grandmother? Master of the Universe! Bow down, bitches!"

He strutted over to the ESCO Sex Appeal Meter, dropped a penny from the cup he kept on top of the machine into the slot, squeezed the handle and let go. The dial spun around to "Overrated."

"What?" he shrieked in mock horror. A second penny produced an even worse result. "Ice Box? No effing way!

"You see, Grandmother," he said, moving in front of his prized automaton, "I get no respect around here.

"Brandy," he yelled toward the stairs, "you hear what they're saying about me? 'Ice Box?' Time to seriously buff up."

Buffing up entailed the most vigorous physical exercise he planned on getting that day, an all-out competition against Popeye's mechanical arm.

"C'mon, Popeye, old man," he said. "Let's wrestle." A quarter produced a scratchy rendition of "Popeye the Sailor Man (Toot Toot)."

"I ain't no 'Spinach Eater' or no 'Bluto Beater,'" he said to the assembled machines, those being Popeye's two most difficult levels. "How's about a 'Muscel Man' or a 'Spiflicator?' he mused, considering less difficult levels he knew he was not up to. "Probably not," he concluded.

"Come on, sailor man. You want a piece of me? Here comes 'Sardine' or maybe even 'Junior Popeye.'"

Reluctantly, Popeye gave up "Sardine." Earle scowled and inserted another quarter. The outcome was even worse.

"Not even 'Sardine' this time? Shit! None of the above? Not wasting any more quarters on you, Sailor Man."

"I definitely need more power credits," he said, heading for the kitchen to refill his coffee.

"What? No spinach? Well, okay then. Another chocolate donut if you insist!

"Now then, Grandmother," he said returning to his arcade. "What you got to say for yourself this morning, you gorgeous old woman you?" He dropped a nickel in the slot.

"Grandmother's Predictions" moved through her elegant routine, pausing her hand over the King of Pentacles. His fortune dropped into the "Your Answer Is Here" slot.

Grandmother's Predictions

A wise old owl sat on an oak
The more he sat the less he spoke
The less he spoke the more he heard
Why can't you be like this wise old Bird?
Yes, my friend your greatest fault
 is that you talk too much. Learn to
keep a secret. A friend will urge you to
take a trip. Don't do it. Your best
interest lies in staying at home.

I'm depending upon your good sense
to lead you on the right path.

Drop Another Nickel in the Slot
and I Will Tell You More

"Grandmother, Old Girl, you're going to bankrupt me with all these nickels," Earle chuckled. He couldn't resist another go.

Grandmother's Predictions

Oh speed on. Speed on my little dove.
Carry a message to the one I love.
Tho a cruel fate has us two parted
I know that the future has in store
Greater happiness forever more.

You are an imaginative person given
to exclaim in ecstasy if things please you.

Drop Another Nickel in the Slot
and I Will Tell You More

"Wise Old Owls? Little Doves? Brandykins, I think Grandmother's flipping me the bird."

He chuckled at his own wit, making his way upstairs to his bedroom.

"She's right about that last thing, though. I'm definitely ready to exclaim in ecstasy if things please me. Ecstasy, here I come! I hope you're ready to please me, Brandy. You just put me to sleep last night, you naughty girl," he giggled.

Earle crawled into bed with Brandy. She did everything he wanted. That's one of the things he liked most about her. And when he was finished, he fell headlong into post-coital dreamland, despite the sugar-bomb chocolate donuts plus three mugs of coffee.

When he crawled out of bed it was approaching noon. He remembered he had promised to meet Noah Meltnick for lunch. Noah was a colleague who still worked at *Musée Mécanique* and was one of the few remaining people in Earle's life, now that he was retired.

He hung Brandy up on the tripod, pulled on some clothes and requested an Uber on his cell phone. A few minutes later, he met Noah at "The Dancing Crab" on Pier 45.

"You're serious?" Noah said, looking up from his Crab Louis when Earle told him the news. "An authentic 1929 'Cleveland Grandma'?"

"The original item, restored by yours truly, complete with

a deck of old-timey fortunes," said Earle. "Wanna come over and meet her?"

Noah glanced at his watch. "I have to get back to work. I'm closing up tonight, but I could be at your place after that, say 9:00 or 9:30?"

"Works for me," Earle said.

When the check came, Noah took out his phone and punched up his Venmo app. "I got it," Earle said.

"You sure?"

"Yeah. No worries. Grandfather's money."

"Okay. I'll bring over a bottle of something tonight. I still can't believe it. An original 'Cleveland Grandma.' You're one lucky bastard," he said.

"Ain't it the truth?" Earle said. "See ya later."

Noah was at Earle's door at nine o'clock sharp carrying a bottle of Old Grand-Dad 100. "Old Grand-Dad for the Cleveland Grandma," he said when Earle opened the door. It was just the sort of wit he thought Earle would appreciate.

Sure enough, Earle grabbed the bottle and cradled it in his arms, waltzing around the arcade as if it were his dance partner. He presented it with an elaborate flourish to "Grandmother's Predictions."

"Grandmother," he intoned with mock solemnity, "may I present Old Grand-Dad."

"How do you do, Mr. Grand-Dad," he replied in an exaggerated falsetto.

"And Grand-Dad," he changed voices again, "may I introduce the lovely 'Grandmother's Predictions' who, rumor has it, hails from the William Gent Vending Company in Cleveland, Ohio; born sometime in 1929, although as a well-bred lady she would never discuss her age."

"She's a stunner," said Noah with genuine admiration. "The restoration is exquisite. I love the clothing and the jewelry."

"Here," Earle said, setting the bottle down. "Take a little peek under her skirt if you'd like." He opened the service panel on the cabinet exposing the automaton's machinery. "You two get acquainted," he said. "I'll get us some glasses. I gotta pee first, though."

Noah had always been envious of Earle's collection and the inherited wealth that permitted him to acquire these rare pieces. He loved his work at the *Musée Mécanique* but he was pushing sixty and there was scant chance he would be retiring any time soon. Noah examined the automaton's mechanisms. They had been as carefully restored as the Grandmother mannequin herself. Noah had taught Earle a lot about these old machines and Earle had been an apt pupil.

He looked around the arcade and at the machines Earle had so expertly restored. Like Noah, Earle understood exactly what they needed to keep them humming. But Earle seemed to be connected to them, and their makers, on some deeper level than most of his colleagues.

Noah had been sorry to see Earle leave *Musée Mécanique*. Most of Earle's colleagues had not. They found Earle crude, insensitive, and largely devoid of social graces.

His hygiene was less than stellar, and he had virtually no ability to empathize with anyone. Still, Noah found Earle intriguing.

He continued to poke around the arcade, waiting for Earle to return. The clamshell Mutoscopes, with their ornately painted and gilded cast iron housings, were Noah's favorites. He dreamed of owning one, but the last time he checked on line, Mutoscopes like Earle's went for north of $20,000.

Of course, it was the reels with their window into the past that made the Mutoscopes so enticing. Vintage Babe Ruth and Charlie Chaplin or flickers of the great 1906 San Francisco Earthquake were guaranteed to entertain. But the Mutoscopes really existed to display naughty peeps.

The old peeps still had a certain charm. The naked ladies in "Women's Night in the Harem" or the "Artist and Model" might have been racy enough to get your grandfather's motor revving, but by today's standards they were tame. The models looked demure, almost innocent.

Noah wasn't exactly shocked when he turned the crank on one of the cast iron beauties and encountered one of Earle's more modern home-made porn reels. He couldn't fathom why anyone would go to all the work of converting a run-of-the mill money shot downloaded from PornHub into a Mutoscope reel. Then again, there were a lot of things he didn't understand about Earle, including why he chose to share his bed with a hyper-realistic sex doll rather than a warm cuddly girlfriend.

Earle returned to the arcade with a couple of glasses and some ice. "Here's to Old Grand-Dad and the Cleveland Grandma," he said, pouring three fingers into his own glass and handing the bottle to Noah.

"A toast to two legends in their own time," said Noah. "Cheers!"

Old Grand-Dad 100 is not one of those Kentucky bourbons for the faint of heart. But tonight, Earle and Noah were neither faint-hearted nor solicitous of their livers. The bottle was two-thirds gone by midnight when Noah phoned up an Uber, finally making good on his promise to head home after finishing one last drink.

Earle locked up behind Noah and shucked off his clothes in the arcade, leaving them on the floor where they landed.

"So, Grandmother, some party, hey?" he slurred. He was still just coordinated enough to put a nickel in the slot.

Grandmother obliged in her usual fashion. She looked straight at Earle as her hand came to rest over the Devil card. Somehow, though, her eyes looked different. More earnest. Perhaps even a little put out. The fortune dropped into the slot.

Grandmother's Predictions

"Naked came I out of my mother's womb," said
the Prophet Job, " and naked shall I return thither."

Grandmother cradled you lovingly when you emerged
naked into the world and instructed you as a growing boy
in the display of proper modesty. When Grandmother
discovered you swimming naked in the pond with
the neighbor's daughter did she not guide you swiftly
back to the narrow path? Now that you are a man you have
lost all sense of propriety. You commit the sin of Onan
in Grandmother's presence as if you were a
naughty child. Grandmother grieves for the children
that will not be born from the seed you spill with a
lifeless mannequin.

Cease this Devilish behavior and turn towards the Light.

Drop Another Nickel in the Slot
and I will Tell You More

"What the fuck?" said Earle. "What kind of sick shit is this! This has to be Noah's doing. There's no other explanation. Noah must have done this while I was in the bathroom."

Actually, once you get over the shock, it's really pretty funny, Earle thought. *I wonder what else he sneaked in there.* He fumbled with the key and opened the cabinet. He removed the stack of fortunes from the dispenser and flipped through them one by one. There was nothing new, just the original fortunes that came with "Grandmother's Predictions."

Earle replaced the cards and closed the cabinet.

"Brandy," he shouted, leaving the arcade and weaving his way toward the stairs, "Did you catch all of that? Fucking Noah! What an asshole!"

A mechanical whirring from the arcade stopped Earle dead in his tracks. He turned around, went back into the arcade and stood transfixed by "Grandmother's Predictions."

Grandmother was not finished with him, nickel be damned.

She was moving her head up and down, from side to side, her chest breathing in and out, her hand moving back and forth over the cards.

Grandmother's hand hovered over the Judgment card and stopped. She fixed Earle in her beseeching gaze. Another fortune dropped into the slot. Earl hesitated for a moment, then retrieved the card.

Grandmother's Predictions

"What do you think?" asks Saint Matthew.

If a man owns a hundred sheep and one

wanders away will he not leave the ninety

and nine on the hills to look for the one

that is lost? Poor lost lamb! Why do you
stray so far from the flock? You are
enslaved by unholy passions. Your idleness
and perverted lust will not bring
Grandmother more lambs.

Turn, turn away from your selfish wandering,
lost lamb, and hasten back to the fold.

Drop Another Nickel in the Slot
and I Will Tell You More

Earle was mute with terror. He dropped the fortune on
the floor and yanked Grandmother's power cord from its wall
socket. He stood there, cord in hand, staring bleary-eyed at
the unplugged automaton, trying to understand the madness
engulfing him.

This could not be happening. "Grandmother's Predictions"
was a machine. If there was anything Earle understood it was
machines and he did not understand this.

Grandmother jumped back to life, her head and chest moving as before, her hand stopping above the Hanged Man card.
She looked at Earle, her eyes compassionate. Earle looked at
the plug he was holding. The fortune dropped into the slot.

Earle stood frozen to the floor, unable to retrieve the fortune. No matter. Grandmother was speaking it aloud, her quiet
cadences measured and pedagogical, her inflections tuned
for the ears of a small child, one for whom she had long been
accustomed to providing patient instruction and correction.

Grandmother's Predictions

Oh Dear! The Hanged Man is a very complicated
card but Grandmother will explain.
You know you must move on, but you can't.
You are upside down, running in molasses.
The way you see the world and yourself
has been all wrong. The trick is to right yourself.
Your heart and your feet are as heavy as lead.
You want to run away but you can scarcely
move. Where would you go? It is pointless to
 struggle. You might as well be an insect
stuck to flypaper.

Help is in sight if only you will take it.
A close relative may be of assistance.

Put Another Nickel in the Slot
and I Will Tell You More

Earle's flesh crawled. He was trapped. Fortune cards shot wildly from the "Your Answer Is Here" slot. Grandmother's eyes were turned to Heaven; she warbled a reedy, nasal hymn of supplication, *"Rock of Aaaages, Cleft for Meeeee!"* The other machines piled on. The triple-monkey barrel organ tootled a spirited rendition of *"Give Me That Old Time Religion."* Space Harrier's synthesizer belted out *"A-wop-bop-a-loo-bop-a-wop-bam-boom."*

Popeye's arm swung menacingly to the strains of *"Run for Your Life"* and the flippers on the pinball machine launched ball bearings at bumpers and bells. Laffing Sal overlaid the chaos with full-throated, diabolical cackling.

Earle, drenched in cold sweat, naked as the day he came into the world, tore out of his house and ran down the block, laughing hysterically, stopping under a street light, hugging the post for support.

A neighbor leaned out an upstairs window and invited him to "shut the fuck up," muttering something about "fucking crackheads" and threatening to call the police as he slammed the window shut.

Earle staggered back to his house, too terrified to go back inside, and slumped down on the sidewalk outside his front door, shaking uncontrollably, his deranged laughter interspersed with wracking sobs.

It was there Officers Ravi Gupta and Mariposa Flores found him when they rolled up to his house. A few cautious onlookers had gathered.

"What's going on, sir?" asked Officer Gupta. No response from Earle.

"Have you been drinking, sir? Can you tell me your name?" Earle was of no help.

"Anyone inside the house, sir?"

Officer Flores retrieved a blanket from the cruiser.

"Anybody know what's going on with this gentleman?" she asked nobody in particular. Nobody did.

"Okay then, we'd appreciate it if you would all disperse while we get him some help."

The onlookers retreated a decent interval, but it was all too exciting to go very far. Things like this didn't happen very often in Sea Cliff.

The officers covered Earle with the blanket and Officer Gupta called for an ambulance. Officer Flores knocked on the open door of Earle's house.

"SFPD," she announced. "If anybody's in the house, identify yourself." No reply. She went inside to have a look around, flashlight in hand.

"You won't believe that place," she said a few minutes later when she came back outside.

"He obviously lives alone. There's a dozen or so old arcade machines in there, some of them creepy but nothing illegal. It's all neat and clean. There's an open bottle of booze on a coffee table, pretty much dead, with a couple of used glasses.

"Looks like he's been drinking, but no sign of a drinking buddy or anybody else inside. I didn't see any drugs lying around. Probably all inside him by now."

"Can we ID him?" officer Gupta asked.

"His wallet was on the kitchen table with his keys. CDL says he's Earle Winston Bradlee III. His DOB makes him twenty-seven. I'll run him for priors and warrants," she said reaching for her radio.

"Oh, yeah," she said, turning back to her partner. "There's a really fancy sex doll up in the bedroom that must have set him back a few grand, not that I know all that much about that kind of thing. Thought for a minute we had a body when my light hit it. Hanging up on a stand, right next to the bed."

Officer Gupta laughed.

"Not funny, Gupta," Officer Flores said. "Seems like everyone's some kind of pervert these days."

The ambulance arrived and a paramedic gave Earle a once over. She didn't find anything that particularly alarmed her.

"No obvious injuries but his pressure's through the roof. He's pretty hammered, but it looks like more going on than just that," she said.

"You think?" Officer Flores said.

"Looks like a customer for the Psych Emergency Team at the General," the paramedic said. "You write a 5150?"

"Here you go," said Officer Flores. "One Earle Winston Bradlee III, age twenty-seven," she said. "Apparently lives here alone. Nobody else inside. Didn't see any drugs. Dispatch says he's clean. We're not charging him."

Officers Gupta and Flores coaxed Earle onto a gurney and the paramedic strapped him in for the ride to San Francisco General Hospital.

"We secured the property," Officer Flores told the paramedic. "Here's his keys and wallet."

"I guess he won't be needing his rubber girlfriend tonight," Officer Gupta snickered. Officer Flores shot him one of her looks. The paramedic looked puzzled.

"He's got a sex doll upstairs in the bedroom," Officer Flores said.

The paramedic shrugged. "Takes all kinds, Officers," she said.

"We got all kinds," Officer Flores replied.

When the ambulance arrived at the hospital, Earle was still babbling incoherently. Medical staff drew a tox screen and helped him into a gown. They gave him some Ativan and placed him on ten-checks.

When he woke up the next evening, Earle was vaguely aware that someone, a nurse perhaps, was checking his vitals. He had no idea why.

"They found you naked in your front yard last night, Mr. Bradlee, laughing and rocking back and forth," the nurse said. "They brought you here so we could take care of you."

"Where's here?" asked a still groggy Earle, propped up in a hospital bed, starring at the wall.

"San Francisco General Hospital, Mr. Bradlee. You're in the Mental Health Unit under a 72-hour hold for psychiatric evaluation, but the doctor can tell you more about that in the morning."

Earle didn't respond.

"Meanwhile, let's get you cleaned up a bit," she said untying his gown. "Are you hungry? Need to pee?" The questions didn't make any sense to Earle.

"Let's just get rid of this," she said sweetly, covering him with a sheet and removing his gown.

She handed him a warm washcloth. Earle had no idea what to do with it.

She took it from him and began washing his face and neck gently. "Does it hurt anywhere?" she asked.

Earle turned and looked at her for the first time. He jumped out of bed screaming in terror and bolted for the door only to be intercepted in the hallway by a Psych Tech twice his size.

"Easy now, Mr. Bradlee," the Psych Tech said. "Nobody is going to hurt you."

He restrained Earle gently but securely and maneuvered him back into his room and into bed. He reached into his pocket and pulled out a syringe of Ativan, rolled Earle up on his side, and had the calming injection in Earle's butt before he knew what was happening.

"That should help you relax, Mr. Bradlee," the Psych Tech said, gradually releasing his hold.

"You just try and take some deep breaths, Mr. Bradlee," the nurse said. "You need to lie here now and not try to get up because that shot will make you woozy and you might fall. We're going to take good care of you.

"Come on, now. Lie back and try to relax. You'll feel much

better in a little bit," she said, guiding him onto his back and covering him with the sheet once again. "That's it. Easy does it," she said. She pulled up the side rails. The Psych Tech went on his way.

Earle was spinning. He gripped the mattress and closed his eyes tightly.

"That's better. Deep breaths. Everything's fine, Mr. Bradlee," she said, covering his right hand with hers. "Sorry I didn't get a chance to introduce myself earlier.

"My name is Mary. I'm the Nursing Assistant who will be taking care of you tonight. Most everybody here calls me Grandmother. Maybe it's because I fuss over the patients a little more than they think I ought to," she said with a lilt in her voice, "or maybe it's just the glasses."

"I really am a Grandmother, you know," she said, making idle conversation to soothe him, "although I'm not as old as all that despite my hair. It's been silver for as long as I can remember. I've always worn it up like this too. Actually, I think it was a shade darker before I moved here from Cleveland to go to nursing school back in the day."

She continued his bed bath as she talked. She'd already wiped down both arms and was working her way down his chest.

Earle was staring at the ceiling, eyes glassed over.

"Grandmother predicts everything will be just fine in a few days, Mr. Bradlee. You'll be back in the game before you know it," she said as she lowered the sheet below his navel and washed his belly.

"Now don't be shy," she said, wringing out the warm washcloth again and offering it to him. "Do you want to wash yourself down there or do you need Grandmother's help?"

Earle was catatonic.

"It's okay, you poor lost lamb!" she said lowering the sheet further.

"Nothing to be shy about. As they say, 'We're all naked when we come into the world and naked we shall be when we leave.' Not that you're going anywhere just yet."

Earle had already left the world as he previously knew it. She pulled the sheet up to his neck, covering his chest and abdomen, and continued on her southward journey with the washcloth. Grandmother had the situation firmly in hand.

"Now you need to get some sleep," the nurse said, helping him into a fresh gown and covering him with a clean sheet and a light blanket.

"All better now," she said. "You just rest now, and I'll sit with you for a little while. Nothing to worry about. Grandmother's here if you need her."

Earle juddered, not unlike one of the malfunctioning automatons at the *Musée Mécanique*, waiting for an attendant to unplug him and post an out of order sign.

GRANDMOTHER OF GOD

It is searingly hot today, as if Satan has unstopped the chimneys of Gehenna. The desert air is filthier and fouler than a buzzard's breath. The caves give some respite from the dust and the wrath of the sun but do not provide much comfort.

When I pray these days, I am more downcast than ever. *Elahi* has surely turned his back on his chosen people. The pestilent Romans He has visited upon us are as thick as flies on rotting mutton.

They harry us for sport. When they discover one of our caves, we are forced to gather our meager belongings and flee to another. No matter. We know these labyrinths far better than they.

Our men are scattered to the far reaches of the desert. We women are old now. Most of us are widows and no longer much endangered by the Romans' insatiable lust for blood and sex. In the past, when they would catch us, they would force us to pollute ourselves with each other for their amusement, on pain of death.

But such depravity only bores them now. They long for the inexhaustible pleasures of Rome: the circuses, the gladiators in the arena and the public baths, the nubile slaves and temple prostitutes with whom they can debauch themselves.

We old women now bear helpless witness to an age of abject misery and despair. Rebellions against the Romans smolder and periodically burst into flame, only to be viciously snuffed out. Tales concerning my grandson Yehoshua fuel the zeal of foolhardy rebels and grow ever more fantastic in the retelling.

And thus, I have determined to set down a record of what I have seen with my own eyes and heard with my own ears, a testament of truth which perhaps will die with me in these caves but, if it be the will of *Elahi,* may be read by others in more fortunate times.

I am called Hannah, by some called Anne, daughter of Issachar and Nasaphat of the lineage of David, wife of Joachim and mother of Maryam of Nazareth and grandmother of Yehoshua ben Yôsēp, murdered by the Romans.

When I served *Elahi* as a virgin in the Temple I learned many things from the priests and scholars, among them how to scrape and cure animal skins to make parchment for their scrolls, and how to make ink with the soot from the smoke of oil lamps. These skills now serve me as I write on parchment

I have prepared from goat skin with ink I have made from the substance of smoke and the colors of the earth.

I learned from the priests how to seal writings in clay jars and hide them in the niches of caves so they will not be destroyed by vermin or the elements and will be safe from the Roman occupiers.

For did not Moses the Patriarch show his aide Joshua, Son of Nun, how to take writings and anoint them with oil of cedar and seal them in an earthenware jar? Did Moses not teach Joshua, who defeated the Canaanites in Jericho, how to protect the books of the law that would later be entrusted to him?

Did not *Elahi,* the Lord of Heaven's Armies, the God of Israel, instruct the prophet Jeremiah to take documents recording the purchase of fields from his cousin Hanamel and seal them in an earthenware jar so they would last for a long time? This, I learned as a virgin at the Temple.

Regard these writings that I, Hannah, leave for you sons and daughters of a more fortunate time. They bear witness to my truth.

The zealots and gossips have spread many lies. They have said that I was a virgin when I conceived Maryam of Nazareth, as she was a virgin when she conceived Yehoshua.

They have said that Maryam remained a virgin after the birth of Yehoshua ben Yôsēp, as attested by the midwives Zelomi and Salome, and when Salome inserted her finger into Maryam's parts after Yehoshua's birth to ascertain her virginity, her hand was burned and withered as punishment for her lack of belief. None of this is true.

The gossip these jackdaws spread that Maryam did not suffer throughout her labor and remained a virgin following the birth of the child are falsehoods. I, Hannah, was her only midwife. There was spilling of blood and pain during the delivery of Yehoshua, my grandson, as there is with the birth of every child.

Nor, when we rested in a cave on our escape from Herod's bloodthirstiness, fleeing from Bethlehem to Egypt, did Yehoshua leave his mother's breast and walk on his own legs to confront fearsome dragons and command them not to harm us. Neither did lions and panthers walk with us on our journey, wagging their tails as harmless pups, larking about among the oxen and the asses.

All of these falsehoods and more have the zealots and gossips told about my grandson.

They have said that while he was a babe in Egypt, he entered the temple at Sotinen, in Hermopolis, and three hundred fifty-five idols prostrated themselves before him and broke themselves into pieces. And that Affrodosius, governor of the city, arriving at the Temple with his entire army intending vengeance, fell on his face before Maryam, with my grandson in her arms, and worshiped him as the one true God.

These fools have said that when Yehoshua was a four-year-old child in Galilee playing at the River Jordan with some village children, he made seven pools of clay with passages for water into which he brought a torrent from the river, filling and draining the pools as he commanded. They have said that one of the children destroyed his pools and Yehoshua cursed him as a son of Satan, killing the child with his voice.

They have said that the boys' parents, with a gathering of Jews, raised an outcry with Maryam and Yôsēp and that my daughter admonished Yehoshua not to do such things lest he make trouble for himself and his family. They said Yehoshua then kicked the dead boy in the buttocks and raised him from the dead.

They have said that Yehoshua then took clay from the pools and made a dozen sparrows. When Yôsēp reproved him for unlawfully doing work on the Sabbath, they said my grandson clapped his hands together and the birds came to life and flew away.

They have said that the son of Annas, the High Priest, came to destroy the pools that Yehoshua made and that my grandson cursed him and suffered him to wither and die on the spot. When the child's parents demanded that my family leave the village, Yôsēp warned my grandson that he was turning the townsfolk against him, so Yehoshua lifted the dead boy by the ear and spoke into it, whereupon his spirit came back to him and he revived.

None of these things are true. Absolutely none of them.

What is true is that Yehoshua was a difficult child, disrespectful of his teachers. He was sent away from their schools again and again. He refused to do his lessons and made no secret that he knew more about every subject than his teachers. Yehoshua often told his parents that he was not their son.

Maryam spoke to him. Yôsēp spoke to him. I spoke to him. None of us could convince Yehoshua to cease provoking others with his insolence, especially his enemies among the powerful in the Temple and the court of the Romans.

I repeatedly beseeched him to take care in his words and behavior for the sake of his own safety and that of our family. His response was that he was about his Father's business and that we were not his family.

Yehoshua insisted he was a mortal human and then he insisted he was not. He insisted his father was not Yôsēp ben

Heli but *Elahi* Almighty. He insisted he was God himself made manifest on earth.

"Does that make my daughter Maryam the Mother of God?" I asked him sharply. "Does that then make me the Grandmother of God?"

He smiled and kissed my forehead. He gave me his blessing. He admonished me to be at peace and not trouble myself for him.

He broke my heart.

And so, I sit in this cave and write what I know to be true and what I know to be false.

We Jews are no threat to the empire of Rome, but they are determined to grind us to dust. They have long since corrupted our priests and rendered the Temple a holding pen for the sheep our venal priests have become. The Romans despise us Jews and count it their pleasant duty to make us as miserable as they can without exerting themselves too much.

Many sabbaths have now passed since my grandson, Yehoshua ben Yôsēp, was hideously tortured and slaughtered on a cross at Calvary, a punishment Rome reserves for terrorists and criminals who are not citizens of the empire. My daughter Maryam looked on in horror. She has never recovered. She is utterly broken.

She would not have me stand beside her as her son was murdered— I watched and wept hysterically, from the shadows. Praise be to *Elahi*, the God of Abraham and Isaac— if there be such a God— that Yehoshua ben Yôsēp died after suffering for only six hours. The rabble was disappointed that he died so quickly. The Romans know how to make the ordeal last much longer; sometimes they prolong it for days.

My grandson was condemned as a seditionist by that

outcropping of Roman excrement Pontius Pilatus, betrayed by our own High Priest Yôsēp Caiaphas and his night soil in the Sanhedrin, our corrupt rabbinical tribunal.

If I had been able to advise my grandson before his trial, I would have begged him to keep his counsel, as I have done so often before. But he would have ignored me. He was as headstrong as a goat. It was the arrogance of the Roman blood in him.

Oh yes. Roman blood without doubt. The Romans rape our virgins with impunity. It is their legal right to fornicate with Jews or any other non-citizen of The Empire without consequence of any sort. Even our young men are not immune to their perverse iniquity.

My Maryam was surely no exception, although she denies it. Yôsēp ben Heli was an old man when the Priests betrothed her to him as they forced her out of the Temple on her 12th birthday, before she could pollute it with her monthly courses. And without the protection of the Temple, she soon became pregnant—she says by the breath of *Elahi*. Maryam swears no man, including Yôsēp ben Heli, has ever come into her.

When Yôsēp found out Maryam was with child, he planned to dismiss her quietly and nullify the betrothal, as often happens in these matters. But the corrupt priests couldn't resist an opportunity to meddle once again. They summoned Maryam and Yôsēp to the Temple.

Abiathar the Priest accused my daughter of carnal impurity. Maryam swore that an angel sent by *Elahi* told her that the child was God's own son, the long-awaited Messiah. Yôsēp swore an angel came to him separately and told him the same thing.

Abiathar the Priest forced both Maryam and Yôsēp to swallow the Water of Drinking of the Lord and walk around the high altar seven times. But no sin appeared in their faces and he begged forgiveness from *Elahi* for his wicked suspicions.

Women of my age have heard many stories like this. In a sheep wallow like Nazareth, a twelve-year old virgin like Maryam, sheltered in the Temple since I weaned her in her third year, stands little chance of not being defiled before marriage, whether by her betrothed, a randy shepherd boy or an execrable Roman.

Nevertheless, we love our daughters and do everything in our power to protect them. Honor killings are a way of life among some of our people. That is why her husband, Yôsēp ben Heli, sent Maryam into hiding with her cousin Elizabeth and protected her along the road to Bethlehem.

But I fear all my care for her, her children and my grand-children has come to little. Yehoshua cried out from the cross, *Elahi, Elahi, lema sabachthani?* Those are the words of my forebear, David the Psalmist, and they are my words also: "My God, My God, why hast Thou forsaken me?"

They are the words of my heart, as I write on these skins, anoint them with oil of cedar, seal them in a jar and hide them in this cave to keep them from the filthy Romans.

Elahi, Elahi, why has Thou forsaken Thy people Israel? Why has Thou forsaken my grandson Yehoshua ben Yôsēp; my grandson who believed he was Your son?

Why hast Thou forsaken his mother who now sits mute beside me, mired in grief? Why hast Thou forsaken my daughter Maryam, called by the zealots the Mother of God?

And why hast Thou forsaken Thy servant Hannah, who the zealots and gossips now call the Grandmother of God?

Selah.

GRANDMOTHER,

NAKED

Belinda flashed her temporary parking pass at the Mason College security guard who acknowledged it with barely a glance and waved her silver Prius into the lot. She hadn't expected the butterflies in her stomach. Probably just first-day jitters.

She pulled into an easy space beside a gleaming yellow Porsche 911 Targa. She smoothed her hair, checked her makeup in the sun visor vanity mirror, and grabbed a large tote bag from the back seat.

She took another look at the Porsche and noticed a student

sticker on the windshield. *How can any college student afford a car like that? Must have a rich Daddy.* She locked her car and walked towards the Fine Arts Building, a couple of blocks away.

She knew where she was going. *Plenty of time,* she thought, glancing at her watch. Same place as last week when she had interviewed with Professor Kimura.

The professor's ad on the kiosk outside the Student Union at Lomitas University, across town from Mason, had intrigued her. It seemed like a perfect opportunity. Belinda didn't need the money but she did need something more useful to do with herself than auditing another class at Lomitas.

Auditing classes was one of the perks of being a faculty wife. Her husband, Richard, had been a Professor of International Relations before he was assassinated on the way to work.

That was a little more than two years ago. A sniper, they told her. A professional shooter lying in wait in an office building across the street from where Richard had braked at a stop sign.

It had been a clean getaway. No security camera footage. No witnesses or shell casings. Clearly a professional hit.

Belinda had always known that something like that could happen. Richard had pooh-poohed her, but she knew better. People in Richard's line of work sometimes got killed.

Not his university work, of course. It was the work he had done before he retired and landed the cushy job at Lomitas.

It still seemed unreal. Richard had kissed her that morning and told her a corny joke on the way out the door, as he usually did.

Richard never ran out of corny jokes. "Dad jokes" the kids called them.

No matter how corny, Belinda always laughed.

"What do ghosts have for breakfast?"

"I'll bite. What *do* ghosts have for breakfast?"

"Boo-Berry pancakes!" he laughed.

Both of them were still laughing as he pulled out of the driveway, never to come home again.

Laughing. That's what they had done best together. That and raising their family. The kids were all grown now, successful, with babies of their own.

With the kids and grandkids scattered across the country, the "Dad Jokes" were all hers now. God, how she wished he were still here to tell them.

Emerging from her reverie, she walked up the stairs to the entrance of the Fine Arts building and made her way down the wide corridor. She knocked on the professor's office door.

"Ah, Ms. Matthews," he said, "Welcome. How are you?"

"I'm well, thank you. A few first-day jitters, but I'm really looking forward to working with you," she said.

"So happy to have you with us," Professor Kimura smiled. "I promise, nobody around here bites."

Belinda took a deep breath. "I'll be fine. Thanks again for offering me the job."

"You're most welcome. I'd better get into the studio and get things organized. See you shortly." He left Belinda alone in his office.

The ad Belinda had answered was for a model for life drawing and painting classes, experience preferred. It hadn't used the word "nude" but it wasn't necessary. Life drawing and painting, she knew perfectly well, didn't have much to do with bowls of fruit or vases of flowers.

Belinda's interview with Professor Kimura last week had gone well. He was pleased to learn that she was not a novice at posing nude.

In college, Belinda had made extra money posing for life classes at a nearby junior college. Not her own college, of course. In those days that would have been unimaginable.

And, she told him, she had modeled occasionally for professional artists.

In fact, she had modeled at the Sorbonne when Richard was stationed in France. It seemed a little pushy to mention that, so she hadn't. Professor Kimura seemed pleased to learn she had any experience at all.

Nor did Belinda tell him that she had always been quite comfortable in her own skin. That was no less true now than it was in her youth. Richard had helped with that. She imagined him lying in bed across the room, just out of sight, while she stood naked before the full-length mirror.

She had become grudging friends with the extra pounds and the stomach that was rounder and softer than it had been before the babies started coming. "A matter of some gravity," Richard had joked. As usual, she laughed.

The babes had taken a toll on her breasts as well. "I'll never forgive those little suckers," Richard said. Again, she laughed. Corny always kept him out of trouble.

"You know, Grandmother," Richard said, "You are a ravishing old woman. Either that, or I am the victim of some glamour. Madame, have you worked some sorcery on me?"

Belinda studied herself in the mirror. *This is exactly how a Grandmother looks. At least it's how this Grandmother looks.* The stretch marks attested to her provenance. It didn't bother her that she had logged a couple of surgical scars to keep the stretch marks company. There were the still visible puncture marks from her gall bladder surgery. And the smiley-face scar from the cesarean delivery of their last child.

War wounds, she joked. Richard said she deserved a medal.

Belinda grew up in a naturist family in Southern California. When she first told Richard, he had teased her, nicknaming her *mon petite nudiste.* She ribbed him too, calling him *un vieux prude* even though he wasn't much older than she was and he was far from a prude.

When they first began to date, in Belinda's senior year in college, Richard had just returned to the United States from a two-year stint as a Rhodes Scholar, destined for a career in the Diplomatic Service. She had not known that Richard had been recruited at Oxford by a more clandestine agency. His State Department assignment would merely be his cover as a spook.

Their courtship was intense. Richard quickly proposed and she accepted enthusiatically. Richard told her as much about his job as he could and she guessed most of the rest.

When they were married, the week after she graduated, she was already two months pregnant. A month later, Richard, with Belinda in tow, was posted to Marseilles.

Like all Foreign Service wives, she had been well oriented to her semi-official duties. She was expected to socialize and she received intensive training in how to comport herself.

She was taught how to throw a birthday party and how to conduct herself at a diplomatic affair, whether a formal dinner or a simple luncheon for the other Diplomatic Corps wives. She was schooled how to listen, observe and probe politely for the ordinary minutiae of family life. What were the names and ages of the children and pets? Where did a family like to go on holiday? Hobbies. Schools. Church. Shopping. She learned to be hyper aware of her surroundings. To pay attention to things that didn't quite fit. To be suspicious of coincidences.

And then, of course, she was taught how to report back in

minute detail. This was the way dossiers were constructed. Bit by trivial bit.

In most ways, being married to a spook was not all that different from being married to a used car salesman or any other man. Richard didn't bring his work home with him. It wasn't necessary to get into the weeds about what he was doing. Nor was it desirable.

Still, she knew that Richard's work was dangerous. Nevertheless, she trusted him completely. If he said that something seemed "hinky," one of his favorite words, she had no doubt it was. If he opined that someone was a "good person," she accepted it as gospel. Above all, she knew he would always take care of her. He said so and she believed it. It made it a little easier to live with the ever-present fear that something terrible might someday befall him.

Belinda loved her life in Marseille. *Le bèbè* arrived at *Maternité Saint Joseph* with the help of *une sage-femme*. Richard was not in attendance for the birth of their first child. He was somewhere in North Africa. It was pretty much the same for children numbers two and three. And now he was dead. It all seemed so long ago.

As she mused, Belinda undressed, folded her clothes neatly and placed them in her tote. She did a few stretches to limber up and slipped on a comforting white terry cloth robe and gray scuffs. The butterflies in her stomach had flown away. Professor Kimura had been as warm and reassuring today as he was in her interview last Tuesday when he had offered her the job and gone over the details.

Belinda opened the door connecting his office to the studio. The Professor was finishing up his housekeeping announcements.

"Ah, excellent!" He smiled at her as she walked into the studio. "Our model is here. Model, if you could take your place on the platform, please."

Belinda slipped out of her robe, placing it on the chair reserved for her, stepped out of her scuffs and stood on the platform, awaiting further instruction.

"Let's begin with some 30 second gesture drawings. Charcoal, I think. Work with the side, please, and not the tip. Big gestures on your large newsprint pad. Pay attention to weight and balance. You don't have to color inside the lines."

The students chuckled.

"Work rapidly and remember to have fun. Model, first pose please."

Thirty seconds went by very quickly.

"Change pose, please." Another 30 seconds.

"Again, change. No cheating, students. Move on to the next drawing."

And the next, and the next and the next. Belinda moved through a familiar repertoire of poses designed for quick studies. It surprised her that after all this time her body would remember the litany, as fluid as a carefully choreographed dance.

"Let's take a break, please, Model."

Belinda left the platform, put on her robe and scuffs, and sat down. Professor Kimura circulated among the students, holding up a drawing whenever he found one to be share-worthy, correcting it with his own red crayon.

"OK, good work everyone. Sixty second poses this time."

He glanced at Belinda, his eyes asking, "everything okay?" She smiled and resumed her place on the platform.

"When you are ready."

Belinda allowed her body to settle into a graceful pose. Professor Kimura walked softly among the students, wielding his red Conté crayon as a magic wand, correcting faults in their drawings.

"Excellent," Belinda heard him say to one of them. "Don't louse it up." Several students laughed.

"Change, please."

Belinda felt the enchantment. The Professor's spell cradled the studio like a cocoon, a space where respect, good will and perhaps a little love, among the students and the Professor, held sway.

"Change, please, Model."

A groan of frustration escaped from a student who wasn't ready to surrender her unfinished masterpiece. Shifting into a pose with her back toward the students, Belinda could hear the crinkle of newsprint being hastily folded back to expose a fresh sheet.

"No, no, a thousand times no," Professor Kimura intoned with mock horror after a few moments. Chuckles broke out across the room as the Professor interrupted their concentration. "Lighten up! That doesn't look like you're having fun."

"Change, please, Model. And OMG no to that attempt, poor pitiable soul!" he camped, ripping a page from a hapless student's easel. The laughter was heartier this time.

"If Model sees this she will abandon us forthwith, never to return. Let's pretend that never happened so I don't have to beg Model's forgiveness." He balled up the sketch and lobbed it toward a trash can. He missed.

Belinda could scarcely keep from laughing.

"Change, please, Model."

Belinda shifted her pose, facing the students again.

"Change, please.

"Okay. Let's take a breather."

Belinda stepped off the platform, donned her robe and scuffs and sat down. Professor Kimura retrieved the balled-up drawing from the floor.

"Too good a learning opportunity to pass up," he said jovially, smoothing the drawing, turning it this way and that, pretending to scrutinize it. He held it up to the class.

"Model," he said over his shoulder, clutching the drawing to his body. "Cover your eyes." Snickers.

"OK. Class. Please put down your charcoal and put on your Loathsome Art Critic hats.

"What do you think? Be nice now! We want to elevate art, not destroy souls. That's for your Political Science or Calculus class."

The hapless victim's classmates *were* nice. They pointed out the strengths and weaknesses in the work. They pondered how it might be made better and the pitfalls inherent in trying to make changes. On balance, they thought it wasn't as bad as Professor Kimura made it out to be.

"Curses!" he said, twirling the ends of a non-existent mustache. "Foiled again! The Loathsome Art Critics have won. The Evil Professor is destroyed and Art emerges triumphant.

"Okay. Back to work. Brandish your charcoal and smooth out your newsprint. Model, if you please."

The remainder of the class passed swiftly. Professor Kimura dismissed Belinda for the day and she returned to his office, dressed quickly, and left a note on the Professor's desk letting him know how pleased she was to be working with him.

Subsequent classes went off without a hitch. Belinda looked

forward to the classes and the post-class check-ins with Professor Kimura.

Then, about six weeks into the semester, Belinda received a call from the Professor.

"Ms. Matthews? Haruki Kimura, here. Listen, something has come up on our end that I need to discuss with you. Could we possibly talk when you are scheduled to be here tomorrow?"

"Sure. Professor. Before class?"

"Actually, we've canceled tomorrow's class but we will pay you your modeling fee as usual."

Belinda's heart dropped into her shoes.

"Is there something wrong?"

"Well, yes, there is a bit of a concern, but I assure you it is nothing of your doing. I apologize for being so cryptic but it would not be a good idea to go into details over the phone."

The butterflies were swarming in Belinda's stomach when she knocked on the professor's door the next morning. He answered promptly, greeting her warmly as he usually did. She was surprised to see that he was not alone.

Standing in front of his sofa, from which they had obviously just arisen, was a young woman in a smartly tailored navy skirt suit that screamed newly-minted lawyer and a graying-at-the temples fiftyish gentleman, also wearing an impeccably tailored navy suit, whose dress and demeanor suggested that he was an academic functionary of more than middling importance.

"Good morning, Ms. Matthews," the lawyer said, extending her hand. "Paula Jamieson, General Counsel for Mason College."

"Thomas Sandefort," said the functionary, extending his hand. "Vice-President for Community Affairs."

Professor Kimura offered Belinda a chair. She looked at him

with a puzzled expression. His eyes told her that he had been instructed to leave the talking to the suits.

"Ms. Matthews," the attorney began, "thank you for agreeing to meet with us on such short notice. I'll come right to the point. It has come to our attention that someone, likely one of our students, has posted photographs of you, with unflattering comments, on Twitter."

"What sort of photographs?" Belinda asked, already knowing the answer.

The functionary cleared his throat discretely. "They appear to be photographs taken of you while you were modeling," the attorney said crisply. "There is a link to a brief video as well. Belinda glanced at Professor Kimura, trying to gain additional information, but he did not meet her eyes.

"I see," she said.

"First," the lawyer said, "we want to assure you that the College is doing everything possible to have the compromising material removed from Twitter as quickly as possible. We were in touch with their legal counsel as soon as we became aware of the Tweets and demanded that they remove them immediately. Twitter has assured us that they have removed everything and they are cooperating with us to determine who posted the photographs.

"The College will also be meeting with Professor Kimura to take whatever measures are necessary to see that something like this never occurs again."

The attorney looked straight at Professor Kimura. It was not a benevolent look. "In the meantime, we have asked Professor Kimura to refocus his course while the College evaluates the wisdom of having unclothed models in our art classes. For the moment, we have suspended the life class and are working with Academic Affairs to place students in other appropriate classes."

Belinda looked over at the professor. His eyes were downcast, like those of a little boy who had just been spanked in public.

It was the functionary's turn. "On behalf of the College I want you to know that we regret sincerely that your privacy has been compromised here at Mason. The Academic Dean will be meeting with the Art Faculty to discuss the ramifications of exposing members of our community, such as yourself, to such danger and humiliation."

Danger? Humiliation? So, that's their game! They brought in all this navy wool suiting to shift whatever blame they can onto Professor Kimura's shoulders. Belinda's eyes momentarily flashed anger.

The functionary was not finished. "When we have identified the perpetrator or perpetrators, we will act swiftly and decisively to mete out justice."

Ah, yes. Justice! Brenda could smell the nuclear option. *And let the fires of retribution pour down upon the professor's head.*

The functionary, like his counterparts everywhere, seemed comfortable with cliché. Belinda expected to hear next that the College's thoughts and prayers were with her in these difficult times. But he had apparently run out of platitudes.

"The College also wants you to know that if there is anything we can do to support you going forward, you should feel free to let us know," the attorney said, without a hint of warmth.

Belinda brought her emotions under control. "I assume all of you have seen the photos?"

The suits and Professor Kimura nodded.

"Might I also see them?" Belinda asked.

"Of course," the attorney said, unzipping a leather portfolio and handing her a sheaf of printouts.

They sat in uneasy silence as Belinda looked at the pages. It was instantly clear to her from the angle of the photographs who had taken them. *That over privileged little fuck!* she thought as she read the Tweets.

Paul X. Gauguin
@BadassWheels

I could not unsee this so neither can you. Forty grand a year tuition and all college can afford for art model is Naked Grandma!

Bill Williams
@Skuzzballoo
Replying to @BadassWheels

LMFAO my art prof sez drawing drapery mucho important. NG gots her own drapery. Don't need no more drapes.

Bobby Ray Jeeter
@Dudzapimpin
Replying to @BadassWheels

My hot sister will pose nekkid for $25 dollars. Send money to me.

Humbert Hephner
@Machuredottard

Replying to @BadassWheels

Fap, Fap, Fap. Eewe! Nevermind!!

■ **Feminique**
@Wondrouswomyn
Replying to @BadassWheels, @Skuzzballoo,
@Dudzapimpin, @Machuredottard

U bators prolly never seen nekkid womyn cuz
yo heads allays b up u butz. Nekkid Gramma
a Rockstar posin and all! Good luck wit u
dickhedz.

■ **Bobby Ray Jeeter**
@Dudzapimpin
Replying to @BadassWheels

OK. 10 bucks but we ain't going no lower.
She's a virgin.

■ **Feminique**
@Wondrouswomyn
Replying to @BadassWheels, @Skuzzballoo,
@Dudzapimpin, @Machuredottard

Nuttin help u pervs. U never gittin eny. Dat
why u called jerks cuz dat all u does all night!

On and on it went. Belinda shook her head in a way that
betrayed her amusement. She considered for the briefest

moment trolling the suits, asking one of them to explain the meaning of "Fap, Fap, Fap" but she opted for the high ground.

"Poor @BadassWheels," she said. "Forty grand a year and the furnishings aren't up to his standards," she chuckled.

"I'm not sure I understand your amusement, Ms. Matthews," the functionary said. "We take your privacy very seriously."

"As I'm sure you must," Belinda said. "Actually, I'm chuckling about @Wondrouswomyn's Tweets."

Professor Kimura looked her full in the face for the first time since she entered the room.

The attorney bristled. "Mason College has a zero-tolerance policy toward sexual harassment, Ms. Matthews. We're not about to stand idly by while someone posts pornography produced in one of our classrooms and we're not going to wait around until someone gets raped."

Oh, Great! Warmed-over Robin Morgan: 'Pornography is the theory and rape is the practice,' Belinda thought.

Vice-President Sandefort and Professor Kimura wisely decided to sit this one out for the time being.

"Well, Ms. Jamieson," Belinda said. "I don't see anything pornographic about the photos and I don't think @Badass-Wheels's post amounts to sexual harassment. Body shaming, perhaps."

"I'm confused, Ms. Matthews," the attorney said.

No doubt about that. Allow me to enlighten you, child. "What I see are photos of an ordinary older woman appropriately attired for her job as a model in a life drawing class. I'm grateful, by the way, to Professor Kimura for giving me that opportunity."

"I don't think you understand, Ms. Matthews," the attorney said, not nearly so collected as she was when she convened this meeting. "Even if we are successful in getting these posts taken down, by now I'm sure those images are all over the net.

"They're probably already being shared on fraternity cell phones across our campus and who knows where else. Once photos like that are on the net, they're there forever. People commit suicide over that sort of thing."

Really? she thought. *Some things in life never change. People are still prudes. And afraid of being sued.*

Belinda thought for a moment, reminding herself that it was never a good idea to get involved in a Holy war. In the end, she decided to ignore the sensible advice she had just given herself.

"Those suicides are more than tragic, Ms. Jamieson, because they simply don't have to happen. Nobody believes it's a great idea for kids to send nude selfies to their friends. But they're kids. They're going to make mistakes.

"We really should try and help them understand that you don't have to kill yourself because a so-called friend has betrayed your trust.

"Besides, vulnerable childhood is a long way back in my rear view mirror. I am not ashamed of my body. I'm certain my life won't be ruined by some nude photos lurking in cyberspace.

"Of the millions of photographs and videos of naked people on the net doing all the things that naked people have always done, I doubt that these photos of my body with its ample 'drapery,' as @Skuzzballoo so eloquently phrased it, will cause damage to impressionable minds or guarantee me more than the customary 15 minutes of fame."

"But you didn't sign up to have nude photos posted without your permission," said Ms. Jamieson, "or to be ridiculed by a bunch of slime balls."

"True enough. But that's not Mason College's fault. Professor

Kimura took every reasonable precaution and even reminded me of the obvious, by way of complete disclosure, that in this age of 'connectedness,' he couldn't offer any guarantees.

"I understand why the College might be feeling vulnerable, so let me take one thing off the table. Nobody will be hearing from my attorney. Not Mason College, not Professor Kimura, not even the moron responsible for these photos."

"If Professor Kimura had requested that you sign a consent document," Ms. Jamieson asked, "stating that you would hold Mason College harmless in case of an event such as this one, would you have signed it?"

"I see no reason why not," Belinda said. "It doesn't seem so dissimilar to model releases I have signed in the past."

Ms. Jamieson relaxed a little. She seemed, for once, at a loss for words. Mr. Sandefort thought that was a welcome development.

"Everyone focuses on the model in a life class," Belinda continued. "But people forget that the model's looking back. The model knows who is struggling and who is succeeding, who is skillfully manipulating light and shadow, who doesn't have a clue and who is just warming a seat.

"I'm sure we all know that not everyone who is called "Professor" can teach. But Professor Kimura is truly amazing. I've watched him help his students achieve things they would never have thought possible.

"Of course, he couldn't do it all by himself," she said smiling at Professor Kimura. "Somebody has to stand up there naked, but that's the easy part."

Professor Kimura cleared his throat. Ms. Jamieson looked at him and then at Mr. Sandefort. She nodded her head thoughtfully and stood up.

Ms. Jamieson extended her hand. "Thank you for your candid observations, Ms. Matthews. Let us get back with you in a couple of days when we've had time to discuss this further."

"Thank you, Ms. Matthews," Professor Kimura said, sensing his opportunity to extract Belinda from the lions' den. "I'll be in touch shortly" he said, escorting her to the door.

Belinda paused in the hall. "I mean everything I said, Professor Kimura. Whatever the outcome, I want you to know I think you are amazing." She thought she saw him blush just a little.

The professor stepped into the hall with Belinda and pulled the door partly closed behind him. "You were brilliant in there," he said. "Absolutely brilliant. I'll call you later."

When Belinda got back to the parking lot, she saw the yellow Porsche parked a few spaces away from her Prius.

There was nobody around. She checked for security cameras. All clear. She took her keys from her purse.

Belinda, don't do it, Richard said from somewhere in her head.

Belinda just smiled. *Run along, Richard.*

She keyed a long, ugly gash the length of the driver's side of the Porsche and moved around to the passenger side, exacting additional revenge. There was a satisfying squeal of metal on metal. *"Matching pinstripes. Cool!"*

Belinda snapped a couple of photos of her handiwork with her cell phone and walked guiltlessly back to her Prius. She pulled out of the parking lot, headed for home, thinking how much she could use a long soak in the Jacuzzi.

Twenty minutes later, she parked her purse on the kitchen counter and opened a perfectly chilled bottle of Robert Young Estate Alexander Valley Chardonnay. She poured herself a generous glass.

"Orgasm in a bottle," Richard used to say. Belinda closed her eyes to shut out distraction as she savored the wine. Complex, oozing buttery goodness and kissed with just enough toasty oak.

She stood at her kitchen window for a few minutes, looking at the roses and sipping her wine. Then, she retrieved the phone from her purse, picked up her glass and the bottle and went upstairs to the bedroom.

When the Jacuzzi was ready, she slipped into the bubbling water and submerged herself as far as possible without taking on water. Her phone, on the edge of the spa, buzzed. She surfaced, dried one hand and reached for it. Professor Kimura's number popped up.

"Hello, Professor."

"How are you, Ms. Matthews? I hope I'm not interrupting."

"Not at all, Professor. What's up?"

"So sorry you were subjected to all that nonsense today."

Belinda smiled. For a moment she entertained the idea of snapping a selfie in the Jacuzzi holding the wine glass aloft by way of showing the Professor just how much she was suffering.

"I'm fine, Professor. I hope I didn't make matters worse for you."

"On the contrary. They clearly came in for my head this morning, but you handed them, dare I say it, their butts." Belinda chuckled. "I'm very grateful for your remarkable performance."

"So, we still have jobs?"

"It would appear so. Ms. Jamieson asked that I let you know she intends to be in touch with you tomorrow regarding a proposed model release."

"The things we do for art," Belinda said, with mock weariness. It was Professor Kimura's turn to chuckle.

Come on, Belinda. Carpe Diem! Richard was saying. *He's a good man. Go for it.* The butterflies had returned.

"Are you still there, Ms. Matthews?"

"Sorry, Professor. I was just wondering if ... well, if you might be free later this afternoon or this evening."

Belinda could hardly believe what she was hearing herself say but it was too late for second thoughts. She held her breath. The butterflies were flitting away. She thought she heard Richard laughing. *If you weren't already dead, Richard, I'd kill you myself.*

"I have the evening free," the Professor said after the slightest hesitation. "I had planned to do some painting but frankly I'm not much in the mood after this morning."

"Perhaps we might meet later for coffee or a drink in the atrium of the Steinmetz," Belinda suggested. "I've been meaning to see the Alice Neel retrospective."

"Oh, do you know her work?"

"I've never actually seen any of it. Just photos. Richard told me he had seen Neel's nude *Self Portrait* in the National Portrait Gallery in DC."

"Richard?"

"Sorry. My late husband. He promised to take me there to see it but we never managed it. He said it reminded him of a quote "older me," close quotes. I can see why. Dare we say it, in a "Naked Grandma" sort of way?

"I don't know why we shouldn't say it. It's a stunningly beautiful piece and I dare say Ms. Neel would have loved having you sit for her.

"So, the Steinmetz around six? Will that give you enough time?"

"That would be splendid. I will look forward to seeing the exhibit with you."

"Great. See you then, Professor."

"See you soon, Ms. Matthews."

Happy, Richard? I think you would be. Happy, for me, I mean. I've been so lonely without you, Richard. Haruki Kimura is, as you say, a good man. You've got to give me credit, Richard. I've only ever wanted to get mixed up with good men and they're so few and far between.

The Jacuzzi was still warm and bubbly and there was plenty of Robert Young in the bottle. Belinda refilled her glass.

But now, Richard. If you'll excuse me. I've something to attend to. Belinda was not an avid social media user. She checked Facebook now and again to keep up with the kids and grandkids.

Those who live by the Tweet shall die by the Tweet. Time to die, @BadassWheels!

Using her phone, she opened a Twitter account, following instructions she found on the net about how to Tweet without using her real name. She composed her first Tweet, uploading the photos she took earlier of the vandalized yellow Porsche:

■ **Grandmother, Naked**
@NekkidGramma
Replying to @BadassWheels

Saw this Badass yellow Porsche 911T
today in a college parking lot. Nice Body!

And another.

■ **Grandmother, Naked**
@NekkidGramma

Replying to @Wondrouswomyn

You rock, WW. Happy to hold your cape any day!

She smiled and took another sip of wine. The day was only going to get better.

GRANDMOTHER'S DEVIL

One moment I am vaguely aware that something horrific has happened and the next I am floating in softness, suspended in some soundless warmth. I think I should be terrified, but it seems too late for that now.

I reach out to touch the angel in front of me. I am not surprised that he is blacker than burnished ebony. Or is he a purple so deep, so rich I can't distinguish it from black? I have never sensed a color like this, so powerful, so complex, so pristine.

I am consumed with erotic greed, with incandescent lust. I hunger for this angel to wrap his powerful arms around me, to draw me toward that polished slope at the join of his thighs where mortals would have genitals. I want our bodies to commingle, our souls to fuse.

The angel looks at me with perfect serenity and then dissolves. In his place, a devil has taken hold of my hand.

He, too, regards me with perfect serenity. He is not the unpleasant fellow I had always believed he would be. I presume I am damned, since the angel has abandoned me. I presume this devil is here to oversee that everything goes according to plan with my damnation.

My lust is spent. I feel flushed and I know I am wet, but I am completely bereft of understanding. Nothing makes sense. And it seems not to matter.

I consider that this devil holding my hand is not leading me anywhere. We are directionless, floating here in this pleasant warmth. Perhaps this devil is merely an emissary, a minor demon assigned to a minor sinner. After all, I have done nothing truly evil in my life. I cheated on my husband a few times, but surely that is not completely unforgivable. Besides, he has already forgiven me.

I masturbated regularly as a teenager and infrequently as an adult. I learned at a weekend women's workshop at Asilomar that most women do. They called it "jilling off." It seems like no great sin if it is a sin at all.

I actually did it a few times for my husband while he watched and he said it made him hard. I laughed. "You get hard when the wind blows," I said. He laughed too.

I continue cataloging my sins since I am certain this is what my devil expects of me. One of my girlfriends gave me a vibrator at a surprise 40th birthday party—a sausage party she called it, with male strippers. Of course, I fondled a few sausages. Everyone did, I think, except my friend Millie, who was slightly disgusted.

The vibrator didn't do that much for me but Millie told me she likes hers much better than her ex-husband Charlie's sausage, with all his clumsy fumbling around down there. She hadn't even blushed when she said it. But all of us who knew Charlie understood perfectly. Charlie was the one who helped Millie figure out she was a lesbian.

Strange, isn't it? When we consider our sins, our thoughts go immediately to sex.

I knew, of course, that I had other kinds of sins to my credit.

I didn't pay part of my taxes during the Vietnam War, money that was earmarked for creating Hell on earth. And I've gotten stupid drunk on more than a few occasions and said my share of hurtful things. I've broken most of the Commandments. I habitually take the Lord's name in vain. I don't expect I'll get off easy for that one.

I smoked weed a couple of times, but that's legal now so it probably doesn't count for much. I did mushrooms once during the sixties, or maybe it was acid, I don't know for sure. I'm certain it's inscribed somewhere in a Book of Offenses with gilded pages, bound in hand-tooled leather.

I will almost certainly have the opportunity to repent at leisure, under the watchful eye of my devil.

But really, what did I ever do that was so monumentally evil? How did I merit my own devil, he of the exquisite eyelashes and the full crimson mouth? He of the lithe, lightly muscled body, naked as truth and whiter than starlight?

My devil seems not to be concerning himself with my sins just now, though he surely knows them intimately. Why else would he be here?

He is not exactly silent, but I can't make out what he is saying. But there!

"Grandmother Maya," he said.

I understood that clearly enough, although he did not move his lips or open his mouth to speak. Still, I'm certain I heard him. I who am unable to hear anything. Still, I'm certain he called me "Grandmother Maya."

Telepathy, I wonder?

"No," he makes me comprehend.

"Then what? I do not understand."

"Yes. You do not. It would not yet be possible. But soon you will see, and you will hear."

I am still floating in the soft, soundless warmth and my devil still holds my hand.

* * *

Nurse Derek rapped lightly on the door before pushing it ajar. Corazón, the CNA, had just finished Grandmother Maya's bath and was tying a clean gown around her neck. Nurse Derek fiddled with the IV pole. The monitor made regular, reassuring beeps. They had taken Maya off the respirator a few days ago. Her breathing was regular and unlabored.

Corazón changed the urine drainage bag attached to the side of the bed while Nurse Derek flushed the IV in the back of her hand with saline.

"She looks pretty good for someone who had to be pried out of a wreck," Nurse Derek said. "Lucky she didn't kill that little grandbaby of hers."

There was a good-sized welt between Maya's breasts where the seatbelt had done its work, keeping her from being thrown from the Escalade when she hit a patch of black ice, dodging an oncoming car that swerved into her lane. The Escalade pitched out of control, flipping twice before coming to rest more or less upright against a fence row, 20 feet off the highway.

Her 8-month-old granddaughter, Ellie, securely restrained in an infant car seat, hadn't suffered so much as a scratch. She was safely back home with her mom and dad.

Her husband, Otis, had cracked a couple of ribs and had suffered a punctured lung and a fractured pelvis as well as some damage to his spinal cord.

He had been patched up and released to a rehabilitation facility last week. He would recover but he would not walk again unaided.

Maya had fractured her skull but the surgery had gone well. She had been expected to recover uneventfully; then she slipped into a coma.

Corazón left with the full drainage bag, closing the door behind her.

"Yep," Nurse Derek said sotto voce. "You look pretty good for somebody's Grandma."

He pulled the sheet down to her belly and pulled the gown up around her neck. He went through the motions of listening to her breathing with his stethoscope, but his focus was entirely on her breasts.

"So long as we're here by ourselves," he said breathing heavily, "why don't we just do another breast exam. Like the one we do every night." He didn't even pretend to go through the clinical procedure for chest auscultation he learned in nursing school.

"Amazing," he pronounced, fondling her breasts leisurely. "So soft and inviting, even better than yesterday.

"Let's be sure we check your nipples carefully," he said

tugging at them and twirling them between his thumb and finger in a way that had no professional purpose.

"Nothing, huh? Usually when I do this to a girl I get some sort of reaction, but I guess you're still pretty much gorked out. The perfect patient to play doctor with.

"Let's just have a look at everything else while we're at it," he said, pulling the sheet off her so she was naked except for the gown bunched up at her neck.

"We'll take this cath out tomorrow," he said, tugging at it a couple of times, "so you don't get infected. You can just pee in a diaper, like a baby. We'll have even more fun then, but for now, just a quick peek," he said, touching her vulva.

"Not much hair left down here is there, Grandmother. What did you do, rub it all away? And look at you, you're all wet. Looks like my breast exam stirred up something after all.

"Grandpa's a lucky man but he's not going to be hopping into the sack with you any time soon. He'll be fine, but he won't be much in the man department, if you know what I mean.

"A little more attention up here on the magic bump? I think you like that!"

She shuddered.

"And there you go, over the top," he chuckled.

He heard footsteps approaching and he scrambled to smooth the gown back down over her body

A couple of light raps on the door and the CNA came in. "Derek, she said, "they need you at the nursing station. Is she OK? Do you need me to finish up here?"

"Nope, all done. She's just fine," he said, covering her with the sheet. "Let's go see what they want."

* * *

"Who are you?" Grandmother Maya asks her devil.

He is silent for a moment, then says "Your helpmeet."

"Do you have a name? What shall I call you?"

"You have no need to call me anything."

"Why did the angel disappear from me?"

"Angels minister only to the dead."

"And I am not dead? I am alive?"

"Living and not living. Yet not dead. You are hovering."

"I do not understand."

"Yes. You do not. It would not yet be possible. But you see and you hear, and you will understand."

"Why are you here with me?"

"You have need of a helpmeet while you hover."

"Are you my devil?"

"Yes. Of that class."

"And, will you punish me?"

"No."

Her devil never let go of her hand.

* * *

Corazón wheeled a cart with towels and a basin of warm water into Grandmother Maya's room.

"Hello, good morning, Miss Maya. It's Corazón. How are you this morning? I've come to clean you up and make you more comfortable. Let's get you a bath and a clean gown.

"You're looking better every day. That seat belt mark on your chest is beginning to fade. And you're going to get that catheter out soon. That will make it easier to keep you fresh."

Corazón began to hum, almost to herself, as she set to work bathing Maya.

"I stopped by the chapel over lunch yesterday to light a

candle for you and pray the Rosary. I don't have all that much time over lunch, but I can get through all Five Mysteries in about 15 minutes. My mother always said I prayed the Rosary faster than anyone she knew," she giggled.

"Top's all finished," she said. "Let's do the bottom.

"It looks like we need to get those toenails polished and your fingernails could use a little attention. I'll ask Lucinda if she can do that for you. She's one of our wonderful volunteers. She has her own beauty salon and I'm sure when you're ready to leave us she'll be happy to give you a nice facial and a mani-pedi at her place. Have you been there? It's Lucinda's Day Spa on First Street.

"By the way, I asked Sister Mary Joseph if she could stop by to see you today. I told her I think you are getting ready to come back to us. Such a beautiful day today, full of bright sunshine. It's still cold out, though. Are you warm enough?

"I know you can see me and hear what I'm saying when I talk to you Grandmother Maya, even with your eyes closed. Maybe you can't exactly see with your eyes or hear my words with your ears, but I know you can see and hear me somehow. God gives us other kinds of eyes and ears when He chooses.

"I think you can understand most everything that goes on around you, but you just can't tell us yet. It isn't important how you do that. The important thing is that you come back to us when you are ready. We'll be here to welcome you home."

Sister Mary Joseph, the Hospital Administrator, tapped on Maya's door before entering her room.

"Hello, Maya, Corazón," Sister Mary Joseph said. "I hope I am not interrupting."

"Hello, Sister. I told Grandmother Maya you might be stopping by," Corazón said.

"We've just been chatting while we do her bath. Well actually," Corazón giggled, "I've been chattering away as usual and Grandmother Maya has been listening patiently."

Sister Mary Joseph smiled. What would we do without the Corazóns of the world?

Corazón suddenly turned serious as she tied a clean gown around Grandmother Maya's neck and covered her with a sheet.

"I can't say much to the nurses, Sister, and I know sometimes we're short-handed, but somehow I think Grandmother Maya might like a different night nurse.

"Mind you, Grandmother Maya would never complain, and I don't want to say anything against Nurse Derek, but I sometimes think she's uncomfortable when he's here, especially when he's here by himself."

Sister Mary Joseph raised an eyebrow ever so slightly and nodded. "I'll look into it. God bless you, Grandmother Maya. And you too, Corazón. You two enjoy your chat," she said.

"I hope it's OK with you that I asked Sister to stop by, Grandmother Maya. I told her all about you today in the Chapel, when I was praying for you. She's a wonderful person. Did you know she's a doctor as well as a nun? Not much in this hospital Sister doesn't know about." She pulled the coverlet into place.

"Oh, I almost forgot. I talked to your husband in the rehab facility last evening. I stopped by to see how he was getting along on the way home from work. He says he misses you and to tell you he loves you. I told him I knew you missed him too and we all hoped you would be back together very soon.

"Well, it looks like we're all finished for now. I'll stop back to check on you before I go off my shift. You rest now, Grandmother Maya. Just take it slow and easy, OK?"

* * *

Sister Mary Joseph was worried. She knew Corazón wasn't given to idle gossip. Her "chattering," as she put it, came from a place deep in her good heart. As a physician herself, Sister Mary Joseph knew about miracles and the people who worked with God to make them happen in her hospital every day. Corazón was one of those. But was Nurse Derek?

She scrolled through Grandmother Maya's chart on her terminal. Nothing really seemed to be amiss. Still, the telemetry looked a little off. What was this thing going on with her vitals last night? It didn't look like much, only a brief period of steadily increasing heart rate, blood pressure and respiration, building slowly towards a peak then leveling off for a few minutes, with another little blip before falling again to baseline. All within normal limits. Nothing to be alarmed about or even anything that would trigger a second look from the nursing station.

But wait. There it was again last night, about the same time. And yes, the night before and the night before that.

Sister Mary Joseph knew this pattern. EPOR: Excitement, Plateau, Orgasm, Resolution. The classic Masters and Johnson Sexual Response Cycle. But did women in comas experience spontaneous sexual arousal and orgasm?

She knew that erections were common enough in male coma patients. But what was going on with Grandmother Maya? Why did this pattern appear at roughly the same time every evening since she had been taken off the respirator?

The likely answer gave her chills. She clasped her hands in prayer and began to recite the *pater noster*. She could not finish. The words about forgiving trespassers stuck in her throat.

Sister Mary Joseph was furious. She would assign Nurse

Derek to chart review on another unit until she could figure out what was going on.

* * *

The next morning, Corazón stopped by Grandmother Maya's room to say hello. To her surprise, Grandmother was not alone. The neurologist was talking to her and checking her pupils. Nurses were coming and going. Grandmother Maya had opened her eyes moments ago and cried out in distress.

"*¡Gracias a Dios!*" Corazón gasped, crossing herself, before she was hustled from the room. "I knew you were ready to come back to us!"

Grandmother Maya was confused by the press of people in white coats and blue scrubs. Her devil was no longer holding her hand. He was standing across the room, watching quietly from one corner.

"What is happening?" she asked him, panicking.

"You are no longer hovering," he said.

"Tell me what is happening. What is all this noise, all this light?"

"You will soon understand."

"I am cold. I am afraid. Hold my hand," she pleaded.

"You no longer have need of a helpmeet. Yet I will remain a little longer and finish my work."

She felt someone squeezing her hand, although it was not her devil.

"Tell me what is happening," she pleaded.

"Maya, can you hear me? Squeeze my fingers if you can hear me," the neurologist said.

She gripped the fingers and squeezed them. The light in her eyes was blinding, so she closed them.

"Open your eyes, Maya! Don't go back to sleep. Open your eyes," he said as he switched off his penlight.

She opened her eyes and tried to focus despite the chaos around her.

"Maya," a voice said, "You are safe. We're here to take care of you." The voice was not that of her devil although it sounded safe and familiar. It was not the voice of Corazón which she had heard perfectly while she was hovering. It was not the filthy voice of Nurse Derek, whose unwelcome hands had violated her night after night. It was the voice of her day nurse, the one they called Carlito.

She looked at her devil in the corner.

"How can I see them and still see you too?" she asked her devil.

"Maya," Nurse Carlito said gently "It's okay. You're seeing things that aren't there. They will go away soon."

"You see and hear with two kinds of eyes and two kinds of ears," Grandmother's devil said.

By now, the doctors had left the room.

"Welcome home, Grandmother Maya," said Nurse Carlito, gently touching her shoulder. "Let's get that catheter out and make you more comfortable so you can rest."

He is so kind and caring, she thought, his hands are so gentle. She felt warm again and safe. Her devil watched from his corner of the room.

* * *

Grandmother Maya improved rapidly. Corazón always brightened up her day with a cheerful presence, making her comfortable and fussing over her just the right amount. The hospital arranged for her to Skype with Otis in the convalescent home. "You poor thing," she said to Otis, "you look absolutely miserable."

"I could not be happier," Otis said. "I am the luckiest man in the world. They tell me you will be joining me in a few days, and we can start to rebuild our lives together."

Her devil remained watchful in his corner of the room.

"Corazón," Maya said one day after she had finished her physical therapy and was resting in a comfortable chair beside her bed, "is there a Nurse here named Derek?"

Corazón's heart leapt into her throat. "Yes, Grandmother Maya. Why do you ask?"

"I would like to see him."

"I don't think he works on this unit anymore, Grandmother Maya. I haven't seen him in a while."

"Could you check for me, Corazón? I have something I need to say to him."

"I'll check with Sister Mary Joseph," Corazón said her heart pounding in her chest. "I'm sure she will know."

"Thank you," Grandmother Maya said.

Grandmother's devil watched from his corner. "Why do you no longer speak to me, my beautiful devil?" she asked.

"Your own kind speaks to you and watches over you. Yet, I will watch a little longer."

The next day, as Grandmother Maya sat in a wheelchair, preparing to leave the hospital to join Otis in the rehabilitation facility, Nurse Derek, escorted by Sister Mary Joseph, knocked on her door.

"Hi, Maya. I'm Nurse Derek. You're looking terrific. Sister says you wanted to see me?" he said breezily.

Grandmother's devil bristled in his corner, surrounded by

an aura of pale blue fire. Grandmother Maya's lips tingled, and she could taste his agitation on her tongue.

She willed her devil to stand his ground. He did not move from his corner.

"It's good to see you again, Sister," Grandmother Maya said. "Thank you for coming, Nurse Derek. I understand you took care of me several nights when I was in a coma."

"I did. I'm happy to see you are recovering so well," said Nurse Derek.

Grandmother Maya managed a half smile. "Sister, I wonder if I might have a word alone with Nurse Derek."

Sister Mary Joseph hesitated, looking at Grandmother Maya uncertainly. "I'll be just outside if you need me," she said, stepping into the corridor and leaving the door slightly ajar. Grandmother nodded her understanding.

"So, you're on your way to join your husband." Derek began, his tone bordering on insolence. "What's on your mind, Maya?"

She paused, then looked directly at him.

"Derek, I just want to tell you that everything you have heard about people in comas seeing and hearing things that go on around them is true," she said, her tone measured and level.

"I seriously doubt that," Derek said, his arrogance fighting with his fear.

Grandmother's devil crossed the room, energy arcing around him as he stood menacingly behind Nurse Derek, his fingers flexing in anticipation.

Outside in the corridor, Sister Mary Joseph crossed herself and beckoned Joe Tarnovsky from security to join her, tugging her ear to signal him to listen and cautioning him with a finger to her lips to be silent.

"No, it *is* true, Derek," Grandmother Maya said, keeping

an eye on her devil. "I watched you night after night as you stripped and fondled me when we were alone. It's true my eyes were closed but I saw you as clearly as I see you now. I heard your voice , and saw you arousing yourself, pretending to conduct your nightly exams, stimulating my nipples, your fingers sliding into the wetness of my vulva, rubbing, as you called it, my 'magic bump.'"

Derek went ashen.

"I watched your face, transfixed by my body, contorted by your lust. I felt the orgasms you forced from my body with your fingers. I heard you disparage my poor injured husband as you pleasured yourself. I saw and heard and felt all of these things. I did not understand.

"Why is he doing this? I wondered. But now I understand. I understand it all so much more that you can imagine. And in time, you will understand also."

Derek was silent for a moment. Then he said, almost inaudibly. "You can't prove anything, you know."

Grandmother Maya could no longer restrain her devil. He plunged his hand through Derek's back and grasped the beating heart inside his rib cage, squeezing it until it barely quivered. "Now," he whispered in Derek's ear, "I will drag your soul screaming into hell!"

"No, my beautiful devil," Maya said softly. "That is not my desire."

Grandmother's devil pulled his hand from Derek's body without leaving a mark, allowing him to collapse on the floor. The incandescence surrounding him faded.

"Then my work is finished, Grandmother," he said with perfect serenity, dissolving before her, disappearing like the ebony angel had done before.

"I will miss you, my beautiful devil!" Grandmother Maya said in words only he could have heard, but there was no reply.

Seconds after she heard Derek hit the floor, Sister Mary Joseph was on her knees beside him, administering CPR, trying to coax his heart to beat again.

Joe Tarnovsky yelled down to the nursing station. "We need a crash cart here, *stat.*"

Someone pushed Grandmother Maya's wheelchair into the corridor outside her room. Corazón was at her side in a flash.

"Jesus, Mary and Joseph," she swore. "Are you okay? What happened?"

"He just collapsed," Grandmother Maya told her. "I think maybe he had a heart attack. I hope he is going to be all right. He has a wife and children at home with a baby on the way."

"Don't you worry about him," Corazón said. "If he was going to have a heart attack, he picked the right place to have it."

"Corazón, do you think we might go down to the chapel, light a candle and pray for all of our souls?"

"Of course, Grandmother Maya," she said, taking command of the wheelchair and pushing it toward the chapel.

Half an hour later, Sister Mary Joseph found the two of them deep in prayer. She walked to the front of the chapel, crossed herself and genuflected before the altar, and sat down beside them.

"Grandmother Maya," Sister Mary Joseph said gently after a few minutes. "Your driver is waiting. Let's get you on the way to join your husband."

"Nurse Derek," Grandmother Maya said. "We were praying for him. Will he be OK?"

"He's in the ICU, "Sister Mary Joseph said. "We will all pray for him."

GRAND-MÈRE LE CIGARE

Christmas Eve Eve

At half-past ten on the evening of December 23rd *Grand-mère Geneviève* arises from her chair in front of the Louis XV writing desk in her second-floor office overlooking the barrel-aging room at *Domaine J. Babineaux*. She places her wire-rimmed reading glasses on the desk in front of her, massages the bridge of her elegant nose and stifles a yawn as she walks across the office to the French doors with their antique beveled glass, opening them onto the catwalk running the length of the barrel room.

She turns to the walnut console against the wall to the

right of her desk and tips a generous pour of *Père Julien hors d'age* brandy from a Lalique Owl decanter into a tulip-shaped crystal glass. She selects a well-aged five-inch *robusto* from her humidor and removes the cap from the cigar with a sterling silver guillotine cutter.

She ignites a cedar strip from a candle burning on the console and methodically toasts the foot of the cigar before lighting it. *Grand-mère Geneviève* steps out of her office onto the catwalk and leans lightly against the safety railing, brandy in one hand, smoldering cigar in the other.

Ribbons of blue smoke from the hand-rolled Havana curl heavenward toward the warm amber lights hanging from the vaulted ceiling. The beams overhead are blackened by fungus, nourished by the alcohol vapors stealing out of the porous oak casks below. "The angels' share," brandy makers call it, pilfered by the heavenly host watching over the mellowing brandy.

Grand-mère Geneviève fills her mouth with thick, rich smoke and releases a fragrant blossom into the still air of the barrel room. Scents of chocolate, nutmeg and toasted pecans mingle with complex aromas of vanilla, fruit and leather from the maturing spirits below.

The cigar was made especially for her by old friends in Cuba, stealthily smuggled into California via Mexico by friends of her cellarmaster Pedro de Alvarado. It draws smoothly, as might be expected of a *totalmente a mano, tripa larga* born in the *Vuelta Abajo* of western Cuba.

Grand-mère Geneviève has rolled many such cigars herself, in another time at another place. The pungent smoke evokes memories of a Christmastide half a century ago, memories of life on a Cuban tobacco plantation after *La Revolución*.

And, of course, memories of the young and handsome Julien

Babineaux. He had looked ludicrously self-important that day she first saw him, decked out in a dazzling white linen suit, a *toquilla*-palm Montecristi panama and lustrous cordovans.

Julien was being squired around the *Vuelta Abajo* by a certain Javier Rivas, a minor functionary of the revolutionary government, who was trying to interest him in an expropriated sugar cane plantation. The *Revolución* had been a success. The corrupt regime of the American-backed dictator Fulgencio Batista had fallen. Now, Fidel Castro's fledgling government needed cash.

But Julien wasn't interested in making rum. He wanted to make brandy. Perhaps a tobacco plantation might be more to his liking, the government man suggested. What could be better than making a fine brandy and fine cigars in the same sun-drenched spot, one of the loveliest in all Cuba.

Julien wasn't sold on the idea of a tobacco plantation either, but he agreed to take a look. He wasn't impressed with the land, but he was mesmerized by the *torcedoras,* cigar rollers, working at a beaten-up trestle table in the shade of a tumble-down tobacco barn. There were five of them, all young women perhaps sixteen or seventeen, rolling Havanas while a weathered foreman, sitting nearby in a rusty metal lawn chair, dozed off under a straw hat pulled down over his face.

But Julien only had eyes for *Geneviève.* Genoveva as she was called in those days.

She was fair, for a Cuban girl, with auburn tresses spilling down her bare back, a fading, off-the-shoulders red peasant dress slipping half way down one arm. Her honey-colored thighs, bared by the dress gathered in her lap, looked enticing beneath the tabletop.

"The finest cigars in the world are rolled by the most

beautiful virgins in Cuba," *Sr.* Rivas boasted. "Do you know the *torcedoras* must be virgins?"

Julien did not know whether to believe him or not.

"It's true," he said. "Watch closely and you will see why."

Genoveva saw Julien staring at her. She stared back, transfixing him with eyes the color of molten volcanic glass. She dallied with the six-inch *corona* she was finishing, running her circled thumb and forefinger up and down its wrapper before slipping the cigar beneath the table onto her exposed thigh. She rolled it languidly up and down, the cigar disappearing beneath her dress and then reappearing to make another pass before she returned it to the tabletop in front of her.

"Ah the virgin's touch; her sweetness and purity perfume the cigar," *Sr.* Rivas said.

Satisfied with the cigar's length and girth, Genoveva ran her tongue slowly along the shaft and guided the tip to her open mouth. She twirled the cigar between her lips, moving it ever so slightly in and out, never letting go of Julien's eyes.

Julien turned redder than Genoveva's dress, his galloping heart unable to persuade his feet to move. *Virgin my ass,* he thought.

The girl on Genoveva's left punched her arm playfully and the table erupted in a symphony of giggles, waking up the foreman. "*¡Basta!*" he growled, clapping his hands. "Stop fucking around and get back to work!"

Père Julien was smitten by *la fille aux cigares*. He could think of nothing else on the drive back to Pinar del Rio.

"What do you think about the tobacco plantation?" *Sr.* Rivas asked. "I think the cigar rollers would be very happy to have a new *Patrón*."

"I will certainly consider it," Julien lied. He had already

decided against remaining in Cuba. The Pearl of the Antilles did not seem a promising place to make brandy.

Julien put up at *La Casa Doña Famosa* on *Calle Jose Martí* to review his options. He could not go back to France and his father empty handed. *Why not consider California?* he thought. But he was in no rush. What better place to think things through than *Bar Viñales.* He had grown to love Cuban rum.

Was it his fault if Genoveva and her friends had also decided that *Bar Viñales* was a good place to unwind after a hard day at the cigar tables? Julien watched from the corner of the room as the girls drank mojitos and neat dark rum, flirted with the men and mamboed with each other under the watchful eye of their chaperone, *Sra.* Beatriz.

La señora was not as watchful as she might have been. Rum had become her very good friend.

"*Patrón,*" Genoveva said, taking Julien's hand. "Come dance with us."

"I am not as good a dancer as your *amigos, señorita,*" Julien demurred.

"Come," she said, again locking eyes with him. "In Cuba everyone dances the mambo. I am a good teacher."

She took his hand and coaxed him onto the dance floor. He soon forgot that he couldn't dance. Genoveva and the music made him forget many things for the moment. But somehow, in the whirlwind of colored light and sound, he lost her.

Marisol, Genoveva's roommate at the plantation, sidled up to Julien and whispered in his ear. "*No se preocupe, don Julien.* Don't worry. We made sure *la señora* Beatriz has had too much rum," she giggled. Julien looked across the room to see the chaperone snoozing in her chair.

"Genoveva waits for you next door at *Ristorante Amable*," Marisol said, dissolving back into the mambo.

Julien found Genoveva seated at a travertine table near the edge of the deserted patio at *Ristorante Amable* under the full tropical moon, nursing a *cubanito*. She was wearing the same red dress she had worn the first time he saw her at the rolling table.

"*Buenas noches, Patrón,*" she said as he approached her. She extracted a five-inch robusto from between her breasts. "Shall I make the wrapper tight and smooth?" she asked, hiking her skirts, allowing her knees to part slightly, rolling the cigar on her thigh. She wore nothing under the dress.

Julien watched spellbound for a moment as she rolled the cigar languidly on the inner surface of her thigh before she presented it to him.

Julien passed the cigar under his nose, savoring the aroma, and laid it on the table. "There is a time for cigars and a time for other pleasures, *señorita Genoveva,*" Julien said. "Would you do me the honor of dancing with me?" he asked, taking her hand, drawing her toward him. "I have had lessons from an excellent teacher."

They danced slowly, her arms around his neck, her lips close to his ear, the hypnotic strains of Javier Solis' "*Tu Voz*" enveloping them. Julien's hands explored beneath her dress as they kissed deeply and swayed to the music. He guided her to the table, kissing her neck and bending her gently over the cool stone. He pressed himself against her, holding her as if he had captured a priceless butterfly he feared might escape. When he had climaxed, she took off her dress and reclined, propped up on her elbows, her feet flat against the table top.

He was overcome by her beauty. He kissed her breasts and

his lips trailed down her stomach. She shuddered and he slipped inside her again, rocking together gently at first, then furiously, their mouths finding each other's, tasting the sweetness of Cuban rum and pungent lime, as the music washed over them.

Thoughts of what might happen if someone should come out to the patio flashed through Julien's mind, but he was so enchanted by his beloved that he could not focus his fears.

He needn't have been concerned. Genoveva had made sure they would not be disturbed. She had reminded the proprietor his wife would not look kindly upon his dalliance with her roommate, Marisol, on this very patio last week. Marisol and Genoveva had no secrets from each other, but many useful secrets between them.

The music continued to cast its spell. When they had had their fill of each other, Genoveva put on her dress, fussed with her hair and rejoined her friends at *Bar Viñales*. They woke up *la señora* Beatriz and returned to the plantation. Marisol could scarcely wait to hear the details. Genoveva did not disappoint her.

Julien returned to *La Casa Doña Famosa* and dreamed of Genoveva. There were two fewer virgins this Christmastide in the *Vuelta Abajo*.

A whirlwind courtship followed in the next weeks. Genoveva delighted in flirting with Julien, drinking rum and sharing cigars she swiped from her employer. Sometimes they made love in secluded corners of the town Genoveva knew, but she always returned to the tobacco plantation with her friends and *la señora* Beatriz.

After all, they needed to be at the rolling table early in the morning. Her quota was high. A hundred Havanas a day. And, unless Julien was around, not a single one of them passed over her thigh.

Occasionally they would spend the night in Pinar del Rio. Julien had offered to find a hotel room but Genoveva assured him there was no need. "*La Doña Famosa* will pretend she does not know," Genoveva said. "I will bring her some *coronas*. Everything will be okay." And it was. It was more than okay.

A few weeks later, Julien proposed. A simple wedding in the *Catedral de San Rosenda* was followed by a brief honeymoon in Havana and they were off to France to meet Julien's family in the Charente.

Laurent Babineaux wasted no time rechristening Julien's bride *Geneviève*. A giant among cognac makers like *M. Babineaux père* could not countenance someone with a Spanish name *en famille*. Considering what the Spanish had done to brandy, the idea itself was an abomination.

"She must learn to speak real French, not that *merde* they speak in Canada or Haiti," *M. Babineaux père* blustered. *Et les enfants aussi!*"

Julien promised that *Geneviève* would learn proper French, although he did not know what use it would be in California. And the children and the grandchildren would learn as well. He would steep his heirs in the language and culture of France, especially that of the Charente and Cognac. They would never speak Spanish in front of *les enfants*.

In fact, *Geneviève's* French, picked up from Haitian farmers who worked the tobacco fields before they were repatriated after the *Revolución*, was much better than Julien's Spanish. He found the creole flavor of her speech *tres charmant*.

He could not guarantee she would give up cigars. In fact, he was certain she would not, but there was no reason to upset

M. Babineaux père. It would have to be enough that she would be called *maman* by her children and *Grand-mère Geneviève* by their progeny.

Geneviève was amused. "We have just been married and you are intent on making me a French *abuelita,*" she said. "*Oh, là là, là là, Monsieur!* I am old and ugly, *Monsieur!* A doddering old *grand-mère, Monsieur!*" she laughed.

Julien was eager to build his own distillery. With his father's blessing, Julien and his new bride went shopping for land in America. They settled on *Los Carneros*, a gently sloping expanse of grape-growing paradise in the Napa/Sonoma wine country on the northern lip of San Francisco Bay. Their estate bordered the vineyards of Constantin and Cipriana Vladu, Romanian immigrants whose version of the American Dream was to make the finest pinot noir in the new world.

Julien then hired an architect and set to work establishing *Domaine J. Babineaux.* He also hired a docent, from the *Alliance Française de San Francisco*, to help *Grand-mère Geneviève* become as thoroughly French as possible for a *torcedora* from the *Vuelta Abajo.*

When the barrel-aging house was nearly complete and construction was well underway on the elegant château at *Domaine J. Babineaux,* Julien left his estate and his wife in the care of the Vladus and returned to France to gather the essentials of French-style brandy making.

He bought cuttings for his vineyards: Colombard, Ugni Blanc and Folle Blanche, the prized brandy grapes of Cognac. He ordered a troika of charentais-style alembic pot stills from the storied craftsmen at Chalvignac and contracted for a large stock of costly air-dried Limousin oak to make his aging barrels, ensuring that the *eaux-de-vie* he would distill would be graced by the rich vanilla flavor of that incomparable wood.

He secured precious stocks of aged brandy from the finest cognac houses in France to blend with his own first distillations. Then, he shipped everything to California and returned to his beloved *Geneviève* and *Domaine J. Babineaux*.

* * *

Grand-mère Geneviève blew another cloud of smoke into the barrel room to mingle with the angels' share. It had been so long. Julien had passed away after a brief illness 15 years ago on Christmas Night, God rest his soul. He had requested that his ashes be placed in an empty Père Julien bottle tucked into a crypt behind the altar in the family chapel, a beautiful little sanctuary carved out of a limestone knoll about 50 yards from the château.

There was an empty bottle ready to receive *Grand-mère Geneviève's* ashes waiting in a crypt next to *Père Julien's*. And there were bottles for their daughter Sophie-Claire and their grandson Jason-Julien if they chose to rest in the chapel with *Père Julien* and *Grand-mère Geneviève* until the clarion blast of the last trumpet.

Tomorrow, Christmas Eve, Father Liam would celebrate Midnight Mass in the chapel. Only *Grand-mère Geneviève's* family and their long-time friends, Nicolai and Elena Vladu and their daughter Adriana, would attend. Before Mass, there would be a sumptuous feast for a small gathering in the château.

There had been a Christmas Eve Eve fiesta today for the distillery workers, *Grand-mère Geneviève's* household staff and their families. There had been games for the children and an extravagant amount of horchata, wine and food, with mariachi, dancing and singing. Santa Claus and his elves had arrived in an antique hook and ladder courtesy of the St. Helena Fire Department.

Grand-mère Geneviève had distributed Christmas bonuses and brandy to everyone, right down to the cellar rats, the distillery laborers who made *Domaine J. Babineaux* such a special place.

She finished her brandy and drew gently on her *robusto*. It was time to tuck the barrels in for the night.

"Maintenant, mes enfants." Now children, she said to the resting barrels below.

"Voudriez-vous une petit chanson ce soir? Yes? You would like a little song? *'Dodo, l'enfant?'* Ah! the one *Père Julien* used to sing to you? Very well, but just this one and then you must sleep."

Père Julien used to tell anyone who would listen that his barrels must have a lullaby when they were tucked in for the night.

"The children must know that we love them and are watching over them," he would say. "Becoming fine brandy is hard work and requires a great deal of indulgence and rest."

Grand-mère Geneviève snugged her shawl around her against the chill of the barrel room and began the lullaby *Père Julien* sang to the mellowing brand every night.

> *Dodo, l'enfant do,*
> *L'enfant dormira bien vite.*
> *Dodo, l'enfant do,*
> *L'enfant dormira bientôt.*

> Sleep, baby, sleep
> The baby will sleep very soon.
> Sleep, baby, sleep
> The baby will sleep soon.

> *Dodo, l'enfant do,*
> *L'enfant dormira bien vite.*
> *Dodo, l'enfant do*
> *L'enfant dormira, bientôt.*

"Faites de beaux rêves, mes enfants!" she whispered. Sweet dreams, my children!

Grand-mère Geneviève tiptoed back into her office, pulling the French doors closed behind her. She admired the Tiffany "Wisteria" lamp on her desk, one of many extravagant gifts from her beloved Julien during their life together at *Domaine J. Babineaux,* before switching it off and leaving the office, walking down the ramp outside the barrel house on the well-lighted path past the still house towards the château.

Outside the still house she said *"buenas noches"* to Enrique, the night watchman, who tipped his cap respectfully. There was no need for Enrique to escort her, nor would she want him to do so. She had walked this path by herself many times since *Père Julien's* passing.

Humming softly, she continued homeward. She paused, as she often did, just before reaching the château, to look up into the sky and admire the seven stars of the constellation Orion, the mighty hunter.

Père Julien insisted that the three stars of Orion's belt were actually the Three Kings, or so said the great French astronomer Camille Flammarion. Moreover, the Kings were not named

Gaspar, Melchior and Balthasar, as the priests claimed, but Mintaka, Alnilam and Alnitak, according to the astronomers who knew more about these things than priests.

Perfectly good names for kings, *n'est-ce pas?*

On a clear night, they had sometimes been able to see the fuzzy patch of light to the East, in the faint constellation of Cancer, called The Manger. But not tonight. The air was too damp.

Tonight, *Grand-mère Geneviève* would be content wishing *buenas noches* to *Los Tres Reyes Magos* and savoring the inviting warmth of the château and her bed.

Christmas Eve

The traditional Christmas Eve dinner at *Domaine J. Babineaux* was always a breathtaking affair. The engraved invitations, hand delivered by *Grand-mère Geneviève's* personal secretary, were highly coveted among the denizens of the Napa Valley and environs. Seldom were guests invited two consecutive years in a row. *Père Julien* had established the practice and *Grand-mère Geneviève* saw no reason to break with his tradition.

The exception was the standing invitation extended to Nicolai and Elena Vladu, the proprietors of *Domain Vladu*. The Vladus were longtime friends, having established their cellars at the same time *Père Julien* was building his.

When Constantin and Cipriana passed on, their son Nicolai had become proprietor of *Domaine Vladu*. Julien and Geneviève's daughter, Sophie-Claire, had grown up with Nicolai. When Sophie-Claire went off to college and then to medical school, Nicolai stayed behind at *Domaine Vladu* with his new wife Elena to learn the wine trade from his parents.

This Christmas Eve, dinner would be a much smaller, even more special affair than usual. In all, there would be only eight for dinner, a far cry from the two dozen or more who usually graced *Grand-mère Geneviève's* table. Sophie-Claire and her son, *Grand-mère Geneviève's* only grandson Jason-Julien were spending the Christmas holidays at *Domaine J. Babineaux.* It was rare that the two of them were able to return home for the holidays.

Nicolai and Elena's only daughter Adriana, who had just finished her degree in winemaking at UC Davis, was also back home with her parents and would attend.

Rounding out the guest list this evening would be two colleagues of Sophie-Claire's from her medical school days, Doctors Corbin Levinson and India Hathaway from nearby Sausalito. Sophie-Claire had prevailed upon *Grand-mère Geneviève* to extend the invitation. Despite her misgivings *Grand-mère Geneviève* had agreed. She could deny her darling Sophie-Claire nothing.

Grand-mère Geneviève's family and the Vladus were already chatting in the drawing room waiting for the other guests to arrive. A liveried server offered tempting *hors d' oeuvres* from a sterling tray.

Another was serving *Grand-mère Geneviève's* favorite sparkling wine, Iron Horse Classic Vintage Brut, in Lalique crystal *Ange* flutes. The flutes, with the molded angel head at the top of the stem and delicately etched wings embracing the bowl, would not have seemed out of place among the multitude of the heavenly host swiping brandy from the barrel room, had they required stemware.

In one corner of the drawing room, a superb ensemble from Symphony Napa Valley was playing a Boccherini string trio in front of a freshly-cut balsam fir glittering with tiny lights and Swarovski crystals.

Sophie-Claire excused herself to collect the Levinson-Hathaways, who had arrived at the portico in the limousine *Grand-mère Geneviève* had dispatched to Sausalito to fetch them. Introductions were made all around and glasses were freshly charged.

At precisely seven o'clock, the french doors leading to the formal dining room were opened. *"Mesdames et Messieurs,"* the concierge announced, "dinner is served." *Grand-mère Geneviève* led her guests to table.

The room sparkled with Baccarat crystal and Christofle silver. Gilded chargers reflected the light of the softly glowing chandelier overhead and the flickering of ivory tapers nested in cardinal-red amaryllis blossoms running the length of the table.

A massive cut-crystal Waterford bowl filled with white tulips forced in the *Domaine J. Babineaux* greenhouses rested on the sideboard along one wall. Course after course was presented by servers under the watchful eye of *Grand-mère's* concierge.

Had you been one of *Grand-mère Geneviève's* Christmas Eve dinner guests, you would first have been served an *amuse bouche*, a tiny *rocher* of salmon tartare, garnished with a plump caper and a sliver of crystallized ginger, presented atop a slice of blood orange. You would next have been offered an icy vodka slush, courtesy of friends at the Napa Valley Distillery to prepare your palate for pleasures yet to come, which would have begun with a pair of plump Bodega Bay oysters dressed with pearls of California White Sturgeon caviar nestled in a wreath of angel-hair kelp smelling freshly of the sea.

The soup course was a warm parsnip, leek and apple vichyssoise accompanied by fresh fig and *chèvre* crostini and was followed by a fish course of halibut cheeks stuffed with Dungeness crab.

A flight of extraordinary white varietals from *Grand-mère Geneviève's* Napa Valley neighbors, paired perfectly with each course, sufficed until the crown roast of lamb made its appearance. Elena's Vineyard Reserve Pinot from *Domaine Vladu* showcased the lamb and reigned unchallenged until the warm *frisee* and persimmon salad, dressed with hazelnut oil and champagne vinegar, was served.

Then you would have enjoyed a cheese course, from which you could have selected among half a dozen cheeses from the Point Reyes Farmstead and Cowgirl creameries including the incomparable Bay Blue, Humboldt Fog, and Mt. Tam.

You would scarcely have had room for English Trifle laced with raspberries and pistachios or perhaps *mousse au chocolat* and espresso.

That is, of course, unless you had been following a diet such as that required by the pescatarian Doctors Levinson-Hathaway, in which case the lamb would have reluctantly given way to a cauliflower cutlet sautéed in cold-pressed avocado oil, with similar unfortunate adjustments to the other courses as required.

* * *

When dinner was finished, *Grand-mère Geneviève* invited everyone to join her in the library for brandy and cigars. Sophie-Claire, wrinkling her nose only a little at the mention of tobacco, invited the Levinson-Hathaways to enjoy their brandy with her in the cigar-free drawing room.

At 11:30, everyone reconvened to wish each other Merry Christmas and tuck the Levinson-Hathaways into their limo to be whisked back to Sausalito. *Grand-mère Geneviève's* family and the Vladus walked the short distance to the family chapel where Father Liam Curran waited to celebrate a Midnight Mass for the soul of *Père Julien.*

When the mass was finished, *Grand-mère Geneviève's* driver departed for the rectory with Fr. Liam in the back seat and a case of *Domain J. Babineaux* XO Reserve in the trunk. The fortunate clergy would celebrate many times in the coming year.

The night was mild. Jason and Adriana decided to take a stroll around the grounds. Nicolai and Elena, with barely an arched eyebrow, left on foot for *Domaine Vladu.*

Grand-mère Geneviève walked hand-in-hand with Sophie-Claire, back to the château. Sophie-Claire, who was never very good at hiding her emotions from her *maman*, seemed distraught.

"What is troubling you, my darling? It's a glorious Christmas Eve like the ones we used to spend with your father, God rest his soul, when you were a little girl, before you grew up so fast and flew away to Sacramento to become a world-famous cardiologist. *¡Miras! Los Reyes Magos* are watching over us!"

Sophie-Claire smiled. She had learned how to mask her feelings when she had to give bad news to her patients. Against *Grand-mère Geneviève*, she didn't stand a chance.

"I'm so worried about Jason, *maman.*"

"Why? He seems fine. The lovely Adriana seems to have caught his eye."

Again, Sophie-Claire smiled. Jason and Adriana had grown

up together. As children they were inseparable friends, the vast adjoining kingdoms of *Domain J. Babineaux* and *Domain Vladu* their playground.

"He's flunking out, *maman*."

"Of medical school?"

"He hasn't told me yet, but the Dean's a good friend of mine. He said he wanted to let me know so I wouldn't be surprised or embarrassed. He told me he talked with Jason and that Jason was in tears. He knew he wasn't making the grade, of course, and he was afraid I would be so disappointed in him."

"And *are* you disappointed, my beautiful Sophie-Claire?"

"No, *maman*. Of course not. Pushing him into medical school was his father's idea, not mine. Of course, I'm disappointed for him. I don't know what he will do. Jason sometimes seems so directionless. And he seems so unhappy!"

Sophie-Claire choked back tears and tightened her grip on *Grand-mère Geneviève's* hand.

"Why haven't you asked him about it?"

"I can't. It would humiliate him to learn that his Dean came tattling to his great Doctor Mommy."

"Of course. You were always my wise girl."

They walked on in silence.

"*Maman*, what should I do," she said, stifling her tears as they reached the château.

"There is nothing you need to do, my darling. Jason will tell us when it's his time to tell us. All we need to do is hold him in our hearts until then.

"Now. I think it is well past your bed time. Let's get you ready and tuck you in."

Sophie-Claire took off her clothes and washed her hands

and face. *Grand-mère Geneviève* sat on the bed and waited, holding a well-worn nightshirt.

"I think Santa Claus should be alerted to put a new one of these under the tree or you will soon be sleeping naked again, like you used to do as a child.

Sophie-Claire smiled.

"*Maintenant, mon enfant,*" *Grand-mère Geneviève* said. "*Voudriez-vous de la poesie ce soir?*"

And, as she had done thousands of times before, *Grand-mère Geneviève* sat on the side of the bed and began reciting her child's favorite sleep-tight poem:

> Golden slumbers kiss your eyes,
> Smiles awake you when you rise,
> Sleep, pretty wantons, do not cry,
> And I will sing a lullaby.
> Rock them, rock them, lullaby.

Sophie-Claire joined in

> Care is heavy, therefore sleep you
> You are care, and care must keep you;
> Sleep, pretty wantons, do not cry,
> And I will sing a lullaby,
> Rock them, rock them, lullaby.

"Good night, my beautiful Sophie-Claire," *Grand-mère Geneviève* said, kissing her on the forehead and gathering the covers around her.

"Good night, my beautiful *maman*," Sophie-Claire said, burrowing in beneath the eiderdown comforter.

Grand-mère Geneviève turned out the light and softly closed the bedroom door behind her.

The house was still now. There was one last duty to perform before *Grand-mère Geneviève* could retire. She walked down the path to the barrel house under the sparkling December sky.

When she entered her office at the top of the ramp, she hadn't expected to see Jason and Adriana on the day bed where she sometimes napped, their naked bodies entangled in the sleep of the innocent, their evening clothes draped carefully over the back of the gilded chair in front of her desk. The glow of the Tiffany lamp painted their bodies with a soft burnished light, the color of Indian summer.

Grand-mère Geneviève pulled a light coverlet over them and walked to the console along the wall in front of her desk. She turned to look at them.

"They are so beautiful sleeping there. Just like when they were children."

She turned away to pour herself some of *Père Julien's* finest brandy and select a *robusto* from her humidor.

She opened the beveled glass French doors and stepped out onto the catwalk. She set the brandy on a small occasional table while she prepared her cigar and took the first draws. Then, suspended between heaven and earth, she leaned against the safety railing, brandy in one hand, cigar in the other, gazing upon her children below, turning her head to look at the children on her day bed, once again returning her gaze to the barrels.

Some nights when she looks at those barrels late at night, particularly at this time of year, she is certain she sees her beloved Julien, seated on his favorite cask, the one once filled with the 1935 Hennessy cognac he brought from the Charente to blend with his own first *eaux de vie*. There was just a little of the Hennessy left. Only trace amounts found their way into the current premium blend. After all, some of *Père Julien's* own cognacs were now more than 50 years old.

But tonight, she does not see him. He pays fewer and fewer visits to the barrel room these days. No matter. She is sure she will see him once again, perhaps when it is closer to her time to join him. As much as she loves her family and *Domaine J. Babineaux*, she still misses Julien terribly. It would be lovely to be with him again, laughing, dancing the mambo, making love.

Grand-mère Geneviève takes a sip of brandy and a draw from her *robusto* and releases a blue cloud towards the vaulted ceiling.

"*Maintenant mes enfants. Voudriez-vous une petite chanson çe soir?* Yes, you would like a song? The one about the black sheep? Very well then, but just this one." She begins the song she has sung softly to the slumbering barrels thousands of times:

> *Bêê bêê mouton noir*
>> (Baa, baa black sheep)
> *As-tu de la laine?*
>> (Have you any wool?)
> *Oui, monsieur, oui, monsieur*
>> (Yes, sir, yes, sir)
> *Trois poches pleines.*
>> (Three bags full.)
> *Une pour mon maître*
>> (One for my master)
> *Une pour ma maîtressse*

(One for my dame)
Et une pour le petit garçon
(One for the little boy)
Qui vit dans la ruelle.
(Who lives down the lane.)

The singing coaxes Adriana from her dreams. She untangles herself from Jason and walks out to where *Grand-mère* is singing to the barrels. *Grand-mère Geneviève* offers her the brandy and removes her soft gray shawl, wraps it around Adriana's bare shoulders and pulls the young woman into her body for warmth against the chill of the barrel room.

Adriana nestles in and takes a sip.

"And now my children, one last song and then you must sleep. No fussing, my darlings. Babies must rest to grow older and stronger. Hush, now. I will sing you your favorite:

Qué linda manito que tengo yo,
(What a pretty little hand I have,)
Qué linda y blanquita que Dios me dio.
(How pretty and white that God gave me.)
Qué lindos ojitos que tengo yo,
(What beautiful eyes I have,)
Qué lindos y negritos que Dios me dio.
(Beautiful and black that God gave me.)

"You remember this one, my darling Adriana. My mother used to sing it to me and I used to sing it to you and Jason when you were children. Help me sing to the babies." Adriana and *Grand-mère Geneviève* finished the *arrullo*.

Qué linda boquita que tengo yo,
　　(What a pretty mouth I have,)
Qué linda y rojita que Dios me dio.
　　(Pretty and red that God gave me.)
Qué lindas patitas que tengo yo,
　　(What beautiful legs I have,)
Qué lindas y gorditas que Dios me dio.
　　(Beautiful and plump that God gave me.)

When they finished singing, they shared sips of brandy in silence until the glass was empty.

"Et maintenant, mes enfants," Grand-mère Geneviève said, "it is time for sleep. For all of us."

Adriana returns the shawl and joins Jason on the day bed. He does not stir as *Grand-mère Geneviève* pulls the coverlet over the two of them. She wraps her shawl around her and closes the French doors to the barrel room.

"Faites de beaux rêves, mes enfants. Joyeux Noël!"

Sweet Dreams. Merry Christmas! she says, switching off the desk lamp. Closing the office door softly behind her, she walks down the ramp to the path back to the château and to bed.

Christmas

Christmas morning dawned cool and misty, the winter sun, a weakly glowing orb draped in layer upon layer of gauzy fog. The fog seemed unlikely to disperse before mid-afternoon. Nobody, except *Grand-mère Geneviève* who rose later than usual today at 7:30 a.m. and dressed carefully as she always did, seemed in any particular hurry to get up, although there was general agreement that the gifts under the tree in the drawing room would be opened around 11:00 a.m.

The concierge had illuminated the tree and lit candles around the drawing room moments before *Grand-mère Geneviève* arrived. Soft recorded Christmas music for harp and flute played in the background. An antique tea-trolley, a gift of *Père Julien's* parents, was at the ready, laden with baskets of warm *croissants* and *brioches* and an assortment of *viennoiseries: pains aux raisin, chaussons aux pommes* and *pains au chocolat.*

Grand-mère Geneviève settled into a comfortable settee, her *petite brioche* sprinkled with pearl sugar balanced on a china plate. A server brought fragrant espresso. *Grand-mère Geneviève* had forgone her usual morning visit to the barrel house, not wishing to disturb any of the children who might still be sleeping there.

Sophie-Claire, habitually an early riser, had slept in until 9:00 a.m. She joined *Grand-mère Geneviève* in the drawing room, her tatty nightgown hidden by a pink satin robe.

"Morning, *maman,*" Sophie-Claire said, selecting a flaky *escargot* filled with pastry cream and plump raisins for her own plate.

"Coffee, Dr. Babineaux?" the server asked.

"Hot chocolate if it's not too much trouble," Sophie-Claire answered. She kissed *Grand-mère Geneviève* on the cheek, and sat beside her on the settee.

"Good morning, my darling. Did golden slumbers kiss your eyes?"

Sophie-Claire smiled at the question, an automatic response to a timeless ritual. *Smiles awake you when you rise.*

"Yes, *maman.* Last night's dinner was lovely. And such a special treat to get tucked into bed at my age."

"One's never too old to be properly tucked in."

The server arrived with Sophie-Claire's hot chocolate and a fresh espresso for *Grand-mère Geneviève*.

"Yes. A truly memorable dinner and the cocktail hour was perfect, especially with the music. But, really *maman*. All that fuss with the cigars and brandy? My friends were scandalized that even the young people were filling their lungs with carcinogens and subjecting themselves to the future horrors of various nasty cancers and heart disease not to mention dementia, cirrhosis, seizures, depression, and gout."

Sophie-Claire might have gone on with her litany of pathological possibilities. She had done so many times before for her *maman's* edification. But *Grand-mère Geneviève* did not feel she needed a refresher course this morning.

"These are not, my darling child and brilliant if sometimes vexatious cardiologist, the most elevating of thoughts on a Christmas morning. Just remember, without my cigars, you would not even be here to upbraid me."

Sophie-Claire laughed. The story of *Père Julien's* fall from innocence at the hands of *Grand-mère Geneviève's* merciless cigar-rolling performance was legendary.

"Exactly, my darling child. And unlike your medical friends at my table last night who choose to forego the pleasure of rare roasted prime lamb, I will not die from a lack of joy."

Sophie-Claire had to admit that her friends had seemed a bit disagreeable last night. More than once at dinner she had regretted asking *Grand-mère Geneviève* to invite them. She changed the subject.

"*Maman,* did Adriana stay the night?"

"I believe so, I had the room next to Jason's made up for her and I noticed both their doors were closed this morning as I came down to breakfast. Not that that means very much, since, as we both very well know, there's a door between those rooms."

Again Sophie-Claire laughed. "Remember when they were very young? They were always staying over at our house or the Vladus. When we would go check on them, they'd be curled up in one or the other's bed. I think they thought they were brother and sister."

It was *Grand-mère Geneviève's* turn to laugh. "I didn't know how many grandbabies I had then. Sometimes I'd have two and then I'd have none. Almost never would I have a single grandson.

"The two of them would follow *Père Julien* around like puppies or they'd hide in the bushes, shushing each other and giggling, then jump out at poor Julien along the path as he was coming home from the barrel house and pretend to be dogs attacking him. He'd pick both of them up, one under each arm, and bring them into the house kicking and laughing.

"*Grand-mère Geneviève*," he'd say, plopping them down on the big butcher block in the kitchen. *Put on the stew pot! I've caught a pair of skinny rabbits for lunch!*"

"I remember we told them one day they were getting too big to sleep in the same bed," Sophie-Claire said.

"Why?" they protested. "We'll freeze to death if we have to sleep by ourselves!"

"Well of course they didn't understand," *Grand-mère Geneviève* chuckled. "They went skinny dipping all the time in the pond with a couple of the cook's children and she'd throw them all in that big enameled cast-iron tub in her cottage to clean them up before she got everybody dressed again."

"I don't remember how it all got sorted out but eventually it did," Sophie-Claire said.

"Things do have a way of sorting themselves out if we just don't worry ourselves too much over them and give them a little time," *Grand-mère Geneviève* said.

"And now, *maman,* I take it you are giving me more advice about Jason and his failed attempts to become a doctor," Sophie-Claire said.

"Jason? Who said anything about my darling grandson? But now that you've asked, I have faith that things will work out for him as well. As my *abuelita* used to say, *Si la puerta no se abre, no es la tuya.*

"Your *abuelita?* Funny, my *maman* used to say the same thing. 'If the door doesn't open, it's not your door.' You do realize that little piece of wisdom is currently one of the biggest clichés on social media?"

"Social media? *Mi abuelita* never even heard of social media. How might that have happened?

"Speaking of my darling grandson and my darling Adriana…"

Jason, dressed in his slippers, pajamas and robe, accompanied by Adriana, who wore similar night clothes *Grand-mère Geneviève* had thoughtfully placed in her closet yesterday, were entering the drawing room, eyeing the pastry cart.

"Good morning," everyone said, pretty much at the same time.

"May I get you coffee or chocolate?" the server asked them. "Perhaps some juice?" Both decided on *cafe Américaine.* Pastries could wait for the moment. Pleasantries and good morning kisses were exchanged all around. Yes, everyone slept well. The dinner was splendid. It was the unanimous opinion of everyone present that *Grand-mère Geneviève* was a hostess *nonpareil* and that dinner was the best in memory.

Soon it was time to open gifts. *Grand-mère Geneviève* was certain there was something under the tree for Adriana. Adriana, for her part, had put packages under the tree for everyone last evening with a little help from *Grand-mère Geneviève's* concierge.

Time slipped by quickly.

Sophie-Claire announced that she needed to gather her things for the trip back to Sacramento. *Grand-mère Geneviève's* driver would deliver her in comfort and safety.

Jason and Adriana would be joining Adriana's parents for lunch and a quiet afternoon at *Domaine Vladu*. But first there was the matter of clothes for Adriana.

A phone call from *Grand-mère Geneviève's* concierge to his counterpart at *Domaine Vladu* had already solved the problem. A driver had delivered a bag and was enjoying coffee and pastry in the kitchen, waiting for Adriana and Jason to be ready.

The morning fog had yielded to wispy clouds and a weak sun, although the day was still a bit chilly. *Grand-mère Geneviève* oversaw the various departures with appropriate benedictions.

Jason, who would be spending the remainder of his winter break at *Domaine J. Babineaux,* kissed *Grand-mère Geneviève* goodbye and asked her not to wait dinner. No matter, *Grand-mère Geneviève* thought. Who could possibly be hungry for dinner, although she thought she might later have a cold supper of leftover lamb and *frisee* on a tray in her room.

The château suddenly seemed very empty. *Respighi's Botticelli Tryptych* could be heard in the background. The household staff were discreetly busy with their duties. *Grand-mère Geneviève* decided that the library, with its excellent books and cheerful fire, would be a good place to while away a few hours.

She poured herself a brandy and raised her glass in a toast to *Père Julien,* whose portrait hung over the mantlepiece. He had loved this room more than any other in the château.

She had left the door to the library ajar. The concierge, passing by while making his rounds, noticed her dozing in *Père Julien's* favorite chair before the fire, and quietly entered to place a light fleece over her. When she awakened, night had already fallen and she decided to make her evening pilgrimage to the barrel house. There was always paperwork to do and soon the brandy would need to be tucked in for the night. Perhaps a *chanson de Noël* would be appropriate.

Retrieving her shawl and wrapping it around her, she started down the path toward the barrel house. The night was once again mild and the Christmas sky was bright with stars. She climbed the ramp to her office and, once inside, switched on the desk lamp and began work.

She thought she heard footsteps on the ramp outside and, a moment later, there was a soft tapping on the office door.

"*Grand-mère?*" said a tentative voice.

"Jason, my darling grandson. Come in," she said, opening the door and embracing him.

Jason looked uncomfortable

"Did you have a nice lunch with the Vladus?"

"It was lovely," Jason said, sitting on the day bed with eyes downcast.

"Would you like a brandy, child?"

"No thank you, *Grand-mère*. I think I've had more than enough to eat and drink today, thanks to you and the Vladus."

"Well, there's always room for a little brandy if you change your mind. After all, it is Christmas," she chuckled softly.

"*Grand-mère*," he began tentatively, his eyes still not meeting hers, "I need to talk with you."

Grand-mère Geneviève sat beside him on the day bed and took his hand.

"And have you done something very bad you need to confess, like the time you hid all the eggs when *Père Julien* sent you to gather them, and you told him all the hens had stopped laying?"

Jason smiled in spite of himself at the memory of *Père Julien*'s reaction.

"*Vraiment? Ils ont cessé? They have stopped laying and there are no more eggs? Quelle catastrophe! We shall all starve, Grand-mère!*" Jason had not been able to keep a straight face for long, especially since *Grand-mère Geneviève* had been struggling to do so herself.

"I'm afraid it's much worse than that," Jason said, the smile fading from his face. He turned to meet her eyes. "*Grand-mère*, I'm failing all my classes. I'm flunking out. I'll never be a doctor like mom." He looked down again.

Grand-mère Geneviève listened in silence, her hands folded in her lap

"I don't know what I'll do or what I'll tell mom. She will be so disappointed in me. She was looking forward to me following in her footsteps and now I've completely let her down. I'm so ashamed!" he said, tears welling up in his eyes.

Grand-mère Geneviève turned to him and took his hands in hers.

"Jason. My darling boy. Tell me. Have you been happy studying medicine?"

"I hate it, *Grand-mère*. I'm no good at it. In fact, I don't know what I'm good at. I just feel like I'm a complete failure. I've worked hard at it and tried as best I can, but it's just not working out."

"And have you talked about this with our darling Adriana?"

"Yes. We've talked about little else these past few days."

"Excellent. She's an intelligent and extremely capable young woman."

"She said she wasn't surprised. She said she never understood why I kept grinding away at something like medicine that I hated.

"She thinks I should study painting since that's what I really love. She said I should walk away from medical school before they kick me out."

"That sounds quite sensible to me. Unless, of course, you're walking away from a dream."

"It's not *my* dream, *Grand-mère*. I never really wanted to do this but it's all my father ever talked about. It felt like I didn't have any choice so far as he was concerned. It was so important for him that I make something out of myself, and for him, that meant being a doctor like him and mom.

"But I really didn't do it for him. I did it for my mom. She was so proud of me when I got into medical school."

"I remember talking with my darling Sophie-Claire a few months ago," *Grand-mère Geneviève* said, "when you started school.

"Yes. She was proud of you but she was also worried about you. She was afraid you were doing something your father wanted, not something you wanted. But she didn't want to stand in your way.

"Jason, my darling grandson," she said, putting her arm around him and drawing him closer. "This misfortune you tell me about is merely fortune in disguise.

"You no longer have to condemn yourself to a life you do not want to live. Nobody is ashamed of you. You most certainly do not have my permission to be ashamed of yourself.

"You have never done anything shameful that I know of, at least if we don't count those little jokes you used to play on *Père Julien*, and I see no reason for us to worry about those.

"All that has happened is that you tried to open a door that was not yours. You will find your happiness behind another door.

"Tomorrow, you can call your Dean and withdraw from your program. We will arrange for some of my men to bring your things back here. I shall be very glad of your company for as long as you wish to stay."

"Thank you, *Grand-mère*. I would like that very much."

"We can let my darling Sophie-Claire know of your exciting new plans tomorrow. I'm certain she will be very happy for all of us.

"And I am sure my darling Adriana will be pleased that you plan to follow her excellent advice."

"I think she will be more than pleased, *Grand-mère*. She had another piece of advice for me."

"Oh?"

"She thinks I should marry her."

"And do you plan to follow her excellent advice in that respect as well?"

"I do, *Grand-mère*."

"Does she know that?"

"I haven't told her yet."

"Is there some reason you are here then, talking with me, rather than at *Domaine Vladu* plighting your troth? Can you think of a more auspicious time to have these discussions with my future grand-daughter-in law than Christmas night?"

Jason stood up and extended his hand to *Grand-mère Geneviève* for support as she too rose from the day bed. Putting his arms around her and kissing her on the cheek he said, "I love you, *Grand-mère Geneviève*."

"So you have often told me and I, of course, love you too.

"Now off you go. I must tuck my babies in for the night. I will have cook make a plate that you can warm in the oven when you come home later." *If you come home.*

"Of course, the Vladus will also be happy to feed you, as they have done so many times in the past."

Jason was already on his way out of the office, cell phone to his ear.

* * *

Grand-mère Geneviève closes the door behind Jason and opens the French doors of her office onto the catwalk in the barrel room.

She pours herself a glass of *Père Julien hors d'age*, prepares one of her beloved *robustos* and steps onto the catwalk, leaning against the safety railing, brandy in one hand, smoldering cigar in the other.

She isn't completely surprised to see *Père Julien* sitting on his favorite brandy cask. After all, Christmas is the anniversary of his departure from *Domaine J. Babineaux* and this world.

She is surprised, however, that *Père Julien* turns to smile at her, something he has not done before on any of his infrequent visits to the barrel house. She waves her cigar and smiles back. Then he disappears from her sight once again, joining the angels, she presumes, to claim his share of the ambrosial vapors from the barrels resting beneath the vaulted ceiling.

Grand-mère Geneviève takes a sip of brandy and draws from the *robusto*, releasing a fragrant blue cloud heavenward.

"*Maintenant, mes enfants. Voudriez-vous une petite chanson ce soir?* Yes, you would like a Christmas song? *Une chanson de Noël?* Very well then, but just this one and then you must sleep." *Grand-mère Geneviève* begins the song she and *Père Julien* have sung to the slumbering barrels many times, but only at Christmas:

> *Vive le vent, vive le vent*
>> (Long live the wind, long live the wind)
> *Vive le vent d'hiver,*
>> (Long live the winter wind,)
> *Qui s'en va sifflant, soufflant*
>> (Which goes whistling, blowing)
> *Dans les grands sapins vert.*
>> (In the big green Christmas trees.)
> *Oh! Vive le temps, vive le temps*
>> (Oh! Long live the weather,
>> long live the weather)
> *Vive le temps d'hiver,*
>> (Long live the winter weather,)
> *Boules de neige et jour de l'an*
>> (Snowballs and New Year's Day)
> *Et bonne année grand-mère!*
>> (And Happy New Year grandmother!)

"*Et maintenant, mes enfants,*" *Grand-mère Geneviève* says, "it is time for sleep. For all of us.

"*Faites de beaux rêves, mes enfants. Joyeux Noël!*"

"Sweet Dreams. Merry Christmas!" she says, closing the

French doors behind her. Switching off the desk lamp, *Grand-mère Geneviève* leaves the office, descends the ramp and begins her walk along the path to the château.

Outside the still house she bids *"buenas noches"* to Enrique, the night watchman, who touches his cap respectfully.

She pauses along the path to look into the sky and smile at the Three Kings, Mintaka, Alnilam and Alnitak, watching over her family from Orion's Belt. Perfectly good names for kings, *n'est-ce pas?* she thinks, pulling her shawl tighter.

Grand-mère Geneviève walks the few remaining steps along the path toward the inviting warmth of the château and her bed.

AFTERWORD

I have been asked, "why Grandmothers?" What do these stories have in common?

My answer has been "I don't know," except perhaps that these grandmothers may be observed engaging in a common mission: caring for the world and their loved ones as best they can. After all, Grandmothers are Wisdom Keepers in many of the world's cultures.

Nor do I know where these stories come from. These grandmothers are not my grandmothers nor the grandmothers of anyone I know. Perhaps they are yours. Or perhaps not.

The first of these stories, "Grandmother Sits" started life as a short narrative poem. An altogether undistinguished poem, to be sure, and so a perceptive listener thought when I first read it to her. She rightly suggested it might make a better short story.

Ideas for other stories followed. There seemed to be no end of these grandmothers wishing to be heard. Some I rejected out of hand. Others I fussed with, but they did not make the cut. In the end, I have arbitrarily capped the number at six for this collection.

I want to express my gratitude to the literary journals that first published two of these stories. "Grandmother Sits," was first published in a slightly different version on July 31, 2018, by TheRavensPerch.com. (https://www.theravensperch.com/grandmother-sits-by-h-martin-malin-jr/). I also read this story on KZCT Community Radio, Vallejo, on the April 18, 2019 edition of "The Storytellers," and it may be heard at https://www.californiastorytellers.com/page-4/.

Another story, "Grandmother of God," first appeared in *Meritage*, the 2019 anthology published by Napa Valley Writers, a branch of the California Writers Club.

I am grateful to colleagues who read early drafts or fragments of these stories and offered helpful comments, including those in the Benicia Novelist Circle, the Benicia Writers Workshop and Napa Valley Writers.

My thanks also to a superb proofreader who wishes to remain anonymous.

About my wife, Jan Malin, who line-edited the stories, designed and published the book, not enough can be said. My love and gratitude.

If you enjoyed this book, please consider posting a review on Amazon. Even a couple of sentences would be a huge help!

Thanks and best wishes.

Marty Malin

www.ingramcontent.com/pod-product-compliance
Lightning Source LLC
Chambersburg PA
CBHW071530100726
47908CB00004B/1348